SHIFTER MARKED

SOUTHERN SHIFTERS WORLD

ELIZA GAYLE

GYPSY INK BOOKS

ACKNOWLEDGMENTS

There are many people who go into making each book the best it can be. Editors, cover artists, beta readers, critique partners and good friends. I owe them all so much.

Thanks to the patience and help of friends and family, I was able to finish this book and they helped me make it even better.

SHIFTER MARKED
A Southern Shifters World novel
© 2011 ELIZA GAYLE
All Rights Reserved

Visit Eliza Gayle at:
https://elizagayle.com

Gypsy Ink Books
www.gypsyinkbooks.wordpress.com

Lucas searched beyond the dark, dank cell he sat locked in, looking for the woman stalking him. He couldn't see her, but he scented her fear and the stench made him sick to his stomach.

She paced back and forth outside his door. Her boots squeaking against the concrete floor with every turn, making the kind of repetitive annoying noise that would eventually drive him mad.

Suddenly, she appeared, stepping into the single ray of moonlight coming in through the grime covered window, gripped the cell bars and bared her teeth. "Lucas Gunn, you *will* tell me what I want to know. One way or another I'll find what I'm looking for and you and your clan will suffer the consequences," she growled.

He took a slow, deep breath and used it to suppress the rage eating him from the inside out. There was no way in hell he would ever breathe a word to *this* woman or anyone else about his shifter clan. He'd die first.

He hid his response with a smirk.

"This is getting really old, you asking the same questions over and over, me giving the same answer every time. How many days are we going to do this?" he asked.

"Until you give me the real answers, you sick son of a bitch." An untempered rage surged from her, feeding the animal instincts inside him that he continued to fight. The beast wanted freedom.

So he could hunt the woman endangering him.

He again shoved his rage as far from the surface as he could, and with slow measured movements, he rose from the cot in the corner of his private hellhole.

After a deep breath, and a whole lot of her scent in his head, he edged his way through the dark shadows to her position.

The closer he got to her, the more her emotions pushed back at him, cementing his thoughts about her reckless behavior. Emotion not logic drove her, making her a volatile opponent.

But also an unpredictable one.

The information she wanted was personal for her somehow. A fact he filed away for later as he continued to prowl forward.

When only a few feet separated them he detected something else, the subtle scent he recognized from before but couldn't seem to place for the life of him.

It had become a puzzle for him to solve, and in time he would, because right now, time was all he had.

"You're pushing the wrong man," he snarled.

She jumped back, barely catching herself with her hands before she landed on her ass. He smiled into the darkness, enjoying even that small victory.

2

"I know nothing about the stupid fairy tales you keep going on about. Just because some people like to tell stories and make shit up, doesn't make it true. Shifters," he snorted. "It's still nothing but old Scottish born fiction in the guise of something more. My ancestors have been telling those stories for more than a century." He leaned as close to her as he could get. "Haven't you ever heard of make believe?" he purred, the words edged in steel.

The guard shook her head, her tense facial features, partially hidden under a hat, still betrayed the potent rage she kept barely restrained.

"I already know all about your kind as well as the existence of the other clans with different abilities." Obvious disgust dripped from her voice. "It's only a matter of time before I have what I want shifter and then you'll regret not cooperating." Her lips quirked up in a vicious smile, marring what should have been a beautiful face.

He ground his teeth together and turned his back to her. Her words rang true. Crazy, but true.

Someone had betrayed them, and it was up to him to find out who.

TWO

T he sound of gravel crunching under the tires of Kira's vehicle and the wheel jerking aimlessly in her hands shattered the vision.

Her car careened off the road while her heart jerked with sudden panic as she struggled to refocus on driving and prevent a crash.

She pulled at the steering wheel, trying to regain control and swerve back on the pavement. Cold liquid sloshed at her feet when her water bottle slammed to the floorboard.

Nothing she tried made a difference and her car smashed into the soft sand embankment, surrounding her in a cloud of dust.

What the hell was that?

She clutched the steering wheel tight to still her trembling arms, and racing heart as she sucked in gulps of air.

Not only had she seen what her mystery man had, this time she'd been inside his head and heard his exact thoughts.

Having a man locked in a cell in her head alarmed her enough. But the woman... The hatred that practically oozed from her pores truly frightened Kira.

This was getting ridiculous.

With the onset of her mating call, her normally laser sharp and accurate visions had gone straight past weird and into creepy land with the line between reality and fiction no longer easy to detect. Shit. She didn't know what to believe anymore.

Got to get a grip.

She fished on the floor for her other, unopened bottle of water, which had rolled out of sight. After searching the floor of the car, her hand finally wrapped around the cool plastic underneath the front seat. She twisted the top off and gulped down the water, hoping to soothe the aching dryness of her throat.

Normally the *Tallan*, her psychic ability to see through another person's eyes, came to her when she had specific problems to work through, enabling her to solve situations far more effectively than a normal human.

She'd been using this gift of vision since puberty with extreme clarity, until several days ago when she dreamt of a man she'd never met. A man who reached out to her night after night, gripping her with sexual desire so strong she had difficulty coping.

The man in the cell.

She didn't have many identifying details about him other than what he looked like and the rough timbre of his voice. But there was one thing she did know with every ounce of instinct she possessed?

What he was.

Her true mate.

Had to be. No one else could possibly have that kind of control to get inside her mind again and again uninvited. She shuddered at the thought and shoved it from her thoughts. God she hated being screwed with by fate.

She closed her mind and sifted through the images still burned into her brain. This vision wasn't like all of the others. This hadn't been about being drawn together by some unseen mystical desire, nor did it involve the hot and sweaty sex from previous visions that curled her toes. Those she'd come to expect.

This wasn't dream walking. It was real.

Her mystery mate was locked in a cage, angry and fighting for control by a thin thread.

Could it be true? Was the man she was supposedly destined to join with in trouble? Or was her gift of vision deteriorating faster than expected?

Kira rubbed her temples. Nothing made sense anymore. Least of all a vision of a shifter from an opposing clan.

A shifter. Shit.

A mate she didn't want was bad enough, but a shifter... She shook her head. The situation seemed to grow more impossible by the second. Everyone knew that shifters didn't mate outside their clans.

It wasn't allowed.

If that wasn't enough, the woman in the vision troubled her more. She appeared human and was pressuring him for information on their clans. Something she should know nothing about.

For over a century they'd blended in or hidden away,

making sure humans knew nothing of their existence. They'd lived in the mountains, virtually undetected, and rightfully so. Of all the rules their ruling councils bestowed on their kind, never revealing their supernatural secrets was the one every clan agreed on.

Any argument against this rule was quickly squashed and over the years it had become more like an obsession than a law. There were even death enforcers employed to control what information got out.

She shuddered at the thought of them and the violence they were responsible for.

She'd lived by this code her entire life, although deep down she believed forever wouldn't last. It was only a matter of time before they were discovered and her gut told her that time would now arrive sooner rather than later.

Kira's cell phone rang, making her jump in her seat. She reached across the passenger seat and picked it up. No need to check caller ID, she knew who was on the other end.

"Hi, Mom," she said, trying to disguise her sarcasm.

"Kira, honey, is everything okay? I sensed trouble." She rolled her eyes and inwardly groaned. Her mother used her supernatural ability to invade her privacy far too often.

It bordered on insane.

"No, Mom, everything is fine now. I dozed off and ended up on the side of the road. I guess it's time to stop for the night and get some rest".

"Are you all right?" She heard the tension escalating in her mother's voice.

"Yes, Mom. Nothing to get worried about." Time to

change the subject before she lost control. "What about you? Has anything happened since I left?" She tried to be subtle. If someone had gone missing from one of their clans, the word would spread quickly and a hunt organized.

But until she was sure she could trust her latest vision she had to keep quiet and not let anyone know she suspected her deterioration may have started. Their clan leaders were far too trigger happy when it came to an unmet mating call and the quick descent into madness.

"No, everything is fine here. It's you I'm worried about."

With bitter disappointment, she sensed her mom was not telling the truth.

"Kira, honey I'm still not sure you should have left. It's not safe out there for you."

The more her mother talked the less she needed the Tallan to confirm what she feared. She couldn't hide anything from the woman. Never could.

She knew.

"We've been over this. Out here I get to be the eyes and ears of the clan. I'm perfectly safe."

"I don't trust the humans and neither should you."

Kira perked up. Maybe her mother didn't know. She'd been on her ass to move back home pretty much since the moment she left. Yet another reason she couldn't go back.

Not that she needed another one. Her controlling stepfather was always on a power trip and the fact Kira didn't go along with his schemes made all their lives untenable.

He wanted her mated to someone of his choosing, or worse.

"I'm not going to get into this again," she took a calming breath and prayed for her mother to let this go. "I'm tired and hungry and I need to find a place to stop for the night."

"You're sure nothing else is going on?"

Kira gripped the phone tighter and dug deep for some patience. "I'm positive you worry too much. It's not healthy. If anything changes I'll let you know."

"Well, okay then. I'll expect you to call me when you arrive in California so I'll know you're okay."

Her mother seemed even more paranoid than usual. So not a good sign. "Bye, Mom. I'll call you soon."

As she began to put the phone down, she heard her mom speak to someone, her voice strained. Most likely her stepfather.

"You were right, it's her time—"

Oh, just fucking great.

So much for hiding her troubles. Her too powerful mother had seen right through her and now her asshole of a stepfather was sure to run straight to the Council to inform them her mating cycle had begun.

That bastard would love to see her convicted and eliminated. It would give him the ability to harness more power if her Tallan transferred back to her mother at death.

Manipulating bastard.

The old anger and resentment made her chest ache. Her father's death all those years ago had changed their life and not for the better. Being a female in the clan meant you held the position of power in your family thanks to the female driven Tallan. At least that's how it was supposed to work.

Her father had understood that role, cherishing her mother and standing by her side as a partner and her rock of support. But not all women in the clan were that lucky.

Some of the men refused to accept their secondary positions and went to great lengths to manipulate the women. And the mating call gave them the perfect in.

Females without mates to ground them often couldn't maintain control over the psychic storm going on in their heads. It caused a sort of power bleed that would deteriorate their mental capacity until eventually they became a danger to themselves and others. Once the process began there was very little time to stop it.

This led to women taking less than perfect mates. It could still work, but only if the men allowed the power to flow freely between the joined couple. Many of the greedy bastards didn't, often syphoning too much power that left the woman in pain or worse, including her precious stepfather.

She glanced at the screen on her phone, reminding herself that step daddy dearest would soon come for her or worse.

Her clock was ticking now. She had to find a solution—and soon.

THREE

L ucas Gunn lay staring at the ceiling of his cell. He had so many unanswered questions and his tolerance for this kind of frustration had peaked long ago.

His skin burned and his muscles ached, making him fear his ability to hold back a shift for much longer if he didn't get his adrenaline level down.

For some reason his captors were hell bent on getting him to shift. He knew they watched his every move, he'd found the tiny cameras the first night here, so shifting in his cell was out of the question. There were a dozen of them, obviously designed to film him from every angle. As if they wanted to study him.

However, he couldn't risk exposing his clan, and possibly several more. As a Guardian, it was his duty to protect clan secrets above all else. Which sometimes meant delivering a death sentence to those who threatened their safety.

Now he was caged and helpless with time running out.

Eventually his body would force the shift and it would be him that would be hunted.

Whatever these people thought they knew, he sure as shit didn't want to be the one to confirm it.

The sweltering temperature inside the building made him edgy and the constant need for freedom left him sleep deprived. His cougar stirred, demanding release.

He flung himself from the cot and stripped bare, anything to relieve the oppressive heat that burned from the inside out.

Unable to resist the urge to move, he paced from one end of the small cell to the other. Unbidden images of cool water from a mountain stream, green grass under his paws, and a breeze rustling through his fur rose unexpectedly in his mind. All of which he forced away on a snarl of rage.

Nothing helped.

He laid back down and focused on what he must do. He'd been trying for days to find a telepathic link to one of his kind. There weren't a lot left with that ability, but they were out there and if he caught one at the right moment they had a sliver of a chance to connect. Not that he had a hope in hell of giving anyone his location. He had no clue where he was. His crafty captor had made sure of it.

Then there was his mystery woman. Ever since the binding spell the witch had used to capture him, he'd only found one person to reach.

The sexy redhead that came to him every time he slept.

The only thing he knew for sure about her was the fact that she drove him wild with desire, and if he ever laid hands on her, he'd never let go.

Hell, it was a pretty good bet that when he finally freed himself from this hellhole, he'd hunt her down. If she really existed.

Lucas let down his barriers, opening his mind to any psychic residue that could lead him to a connection with someone able to help before it was too late.

Between the anger of being locked in a cage and the out of control lust being fueled from these constant dreams, his time was running out. He closed his eyes and relaxed his body one muscle at a time, willing himself to drift into sleep. If there was a chance she was real he had to find her.

LUCAS GLANCED ACROSS THE ROOM, *his attention drawn to the beautiful creature standing in the doorway. Ah, she was back. The mystery woman had arrived once again.*

MINE.

Her long mass of russet hair surrounded her head and shoulders, but it was the multicolored highlights of red and gold weaved throughout that shimmered under the soft glow of the overhead lights.

He desperately wanted to run his fingers through the thick strands and watch them dance as the soft silk brushed against his skin.

She wore a simple tank top and denim shorts that would have been ordinary on anyone else, but on her they were exquisite. They hugged and skimmed her lush figure to perfection. Not to mention those tiny shorts accentuated her long, long legs that he pictured wrapped around his waist... He growled.

As she turned to scan the room, he caught a glimpse of a delectable peach of an ass that made him groan with need and caused his groin to tighten.

Compelled to learn more about this woman who kept appearing, he pushed himself from the wall where he lounged. This time he was determined to discover her identity. But every time he saw her he couldn't think past her scent teasing his senses. Or the need raging inside him. He'd never felt this out of control around a woman.

Turning, she met his gaze, and her blue eyes sparkled with recognition and mirrored desire. Was it any wonder he couldn't focus when her need was as palpable as his own?

Neither attempted to break eye contact as he stalked toward her.

When he got close he smiled, hoping it conveyed everything he needed her to know. "I'm glad you're back."

She tilted her head and stared at him, her brows drawn together in confusion. "Do you know why I'm here? And where is here, by the way?"

Her voice flowed like warm oil across his skin and Lucas wondered what it would take to keep her from turning around and walking out of his dream.

He stepped closer, absorbing the heat radiating from her skin and inhaling her sweet scent. Thank fuck for the heightened senses of the cougar. The delicious smell of this aroused female made his body tighten.

"You're here because I called for you." His heart rate accelerated as he spoke. "But I'm not sure where here is either. Nothing looks familiar."

"Then tell me why?" she whispered.

Her eyes glowed with a heady mix of confusion and desire, a

look that stirred his blood, and one he'd become accustomed to during their visits. She wanted him, that was obvious, yet she held herself away from him.

Her lips pursed together, so full and ripe his mind immediately wandered to thoughts of them wrapped around his erection while she knelt in front of him, her hands tightening on his thighs. The image was so vivid he could almost taste her submission.

"Who the hell knows," he said. "Maybe we need each other. Or maybe some things aren't meant to be questioned." He leaned forward and touched his fingers to the mouth that fascinated him. She gasped at his touch. Although to her credit she didn't back away. Instead she faced him with her eyes burning with unmistakable heat.

His inner beast howled for more.

Brushing his lips against hers for a quick taste, Lucas found himself unable to stop from grazing those soft lips with his tongue. Somewhere in the back of his mind, a voice yelled for him to ask for her help, but for the life of him he couldn't remember why. Not when his senses were on overload and a frenzy building inside him.

Then she sighed, parting her lips enough to allow him inside the warm recess of her mouth where he stroked the tip of her tongue with his own.

Tension rippled along his skin when she shuddered in response. He deepened the kiss and grasped her hips, dragging her against his body so she felt exactly what she did to him.

He took her mouth in harder strokes, unleashing all the pent up passion he'd been holding since the moment he first saw her.

She tried to turn, maybe pull away and he slid a hand in

her hair to hold her still. He had no idea why this woman got under his skin, but he sure as hell wasn't going to fight it.

Sliding his hand from her hip, he skimmed up her torso and underneath the thin tank, reveling in all her soft, smooth skin. Pulling back from her lips, his gaze slowly traveled to the swell of her breasts rising and falling in choppy rhythm with her rough breathing.

He closed a callused hand over one mound, growling into her mouth when the nipple hardened in his palm. Holy hell, everything about her fit him perfectly. Heat shot from her amazing body and straight into his. He wanted to be inside her so bad he ached.

A low moan sounded in her throat as she arched toward him, pressing them body-to-body from waist to shoulder.

Mmm. He liked knowing she enjoyed his touch. He rolled one nipple between his thumb and forefinger before giving a tight, testing pinch. His mystery woman twisted in his arms, gasping for breath.

"What are we doing?" she asked.

"What do you think we're doing?"

For a few long heartbeats they stared each other down. He had no idea how to explain the unexplainable other than to admit what he felt went deep. Primal deep. Out of his control.

"Screw it." She grabbed the bottom edge of her tank and yanked it over her head before he could blink. She wrapped her hands around his neck and drew him down to her mouth for another hard kiss. Tongue, teeth and lips mashed together as they fought each other for control.

She had no idea yet who she was dealing with. His need to possess consumed him as he plundered the warm recess of her mouth.

Several minutes later he paused long enough for them to breathe. "Who the hell are you and why can't I stop?"

She shook her head in a confusing non answer a moment before she stole another kiss by thrusting her tongue between his lips for an exploration of her own. Tunneling her hands through his hair, she gripped the strands tight and tugged him closer. The pleasure of her kiss blew him away, licking at his skin until he believed it would burst into flame.

He wanted her, and he wasn't about to fight the connection another second. Thrusting against her, his cock begged for release. The fabric from his pants and hers connected to increase the friction against his sensitive skin, heating him further as a shudder coursed through his body. More skin. He needed to touch more of her skin. NOW.

He reached for the waistband of her shorts.

"Wait." She jerked a few inches away. "At least tell me your name."

"Lucas," he bit out, unable to focus.

He clawed at her damn shorts, pushing them down along with her white cotton panties until they pooled at her feet. He trailed his tongue down her neck, his teeth nipping at the tender skin of her shoulder before closing his teeth around her firm nipple until she yelped. He licked and sucked until she melted against him. Everything about her filled his senses, her sweet taste and especially the heady scent of her arousal in the air between them.

Her knees buckled and he grabbed her around the waist to steady her.

"Oh, God," she whispered.

The heat of her words gave him so much more pleasure than he expected. Watching her writhe and whimper as he worked *her flesh made her impossible to resist. When she spread her legs a little further it was his turn to whimper. He swallowed each breathy sound as he slid a finger between the wet lips of her sex. He zeroed in on her most sensitive spot, smiling against her mouth when her hips rose to greet him.*

Moisture covered his finger, the evidence he craved that she wanted him as bad as he needed her. "So fucking hot," he spoke against her lips.

Her eyes widened at his words.

"Tell me this isn't crazy."

She shook her hand frantically, fear flooding her eyes. "Maybe crazy. But. Please. Don't. Stop."

He smiled and slid a finger inside her. Her eyes got impossibly wider as a low wail filled the room.

"Goddess you're tight."

She whimpered before reaching between them and pulling at the button on his jeans. He grabbed her wrists and stopped her. After a warning look, he slid down in front of her so his head was level with her bare belly. For a few agonizing seconds he simply stared at the indentation, teasing her, before he leaned forward and swirled his tongue inside the tiny button.

"Not yet," he said. Seconds later, he flipped her around and roughly pushed her against the nearby wall.

"What are you—" Her voice trembled.

"Shh. You have nothing to fear from me," he interrupted. "I won't hurt you... at least not more than you want."

His words must have excited her as her inner muscles tightened around his invading finger.

"Like that, baby?" He slid in a second finger and pushed deep. He sure as fuck did. He was fighting against the instinct to shove his cock in her instead of his fingers and ride her rough.

Lucas pushed against the driving need. He wanted to draw this out more than that. Her pleasure was paramount.

But this position...

She was facing the wall, which left her beautiful ass ripe for the taking. He couldn't pass up this opportunity to play. He traced his finger along the seam of her bottom, while his other hand worked his fingers in and out,

"This is mine," he said. He leaned forward and scraped his teeth between her shoulder blades. She quivered underneath him while her heart beat wildly. The sound of her pulse pulled at him. The temptation she offered had Lucas panting for breath as he tried to focus on getting air in and out of his lungs while his body vibrated with need. He grabbed her hair and pulled her head back so he could bury his nose in her neck.

Hot, sweet and slick. He wanted it wrapped around his dick. Her whimpers turned to cries as he gripped the skin of her neck between his teeth and moved his fingers faster. Her climax was coming.

Her muscles tightened a moment before she screamed, flying apart underneath him. His body reacted, swelling to the point of pain. Lucas breathed through the violence rising inside him. He squeezed his eyes shut and savored the sensations surrounding him. When her wave peaked, he increased the speed of his thrusts, sending her over the edge into climax once again.

Then he did it yet again.

When her legs gave out, Lucas lifted her into his arms and cradled her against his chest. She clung to him as her breathing finally slowed and she went completely lax.

"You're so damned hot, I could watch you come all night. And your scent. Fuck, baby. I can practically taste your sweet juices coating my tongue." She tensed slightly. "Relax. I'm not *going to do anything you wouldn't like. This is all about feeling good."*

"You don't even know who I am."

"I know everything I need to at the moment. Your body fits perfectly in my hands and you're so damned sweet. Let go and let me to show you just how far this pleasure can go."

He stood to his full height, drawing her naked body against his still fully clothed form. He should have taken his clothes off but there was no time or patience for that now. Not when all he could think about was getting inside her. He ripped at the front of his jeans until the button gave way and the zipper worked free. Small whimpers sounded in her throat as he jostled them in place. He distracted her by lightly scraping the curve of her neck with his teeth, further inflaming both their need.

"Can you wrap your legs around my waist?"

She didn't say a word, but the next thing he knew she was wrapped around him and he was burrowing into her scorching heat.

"Fuck." He bellowed the word while pulling her down in one rough thrust. Buried to the hilt he felt scorched alive. He couldn't breath and he couldn't move.

Mine. It was the only word that made sense.

When his vision cleared and a semblance of strength returned, he was ready to move.

Then she screamed.

LUCAS JOLTED AWAKE.

"What the fu—not again!" he roared, his chest slick with sweat, his breathing harsh and uneven.

He stroked his throbbing cock, certain he was going to explode if he didn't come soon.

On a sigh, Lucas leaned back and wondered who the mysterious redhead he continued to dream about was. He had to find her, make it real. This shit was making him crazy.

Despite knowing he was being watched, he continued to move his hand up and down his rigid shaft while considering how it would feel if his mystery woman rocked her backside against him as he pushed into her. Warm, wet flesh sucking him inside.

Near completion, the familiar rush of sparks raced across his skin, along with the tickling of fur beginning to come out on his arms. He willed himself not to change, but couldn't stop— didn't want to stop—his orgasm.

On the final image of her wicked smile, his release broke free, subduing the beast. Turning, he looked directly into the camera with a feral grin, knowing he'd once again prevented the change and thus disappointed his captors. He experienced a moment of relief, but it wouldn't last for long. He needed to escape soon and find this woman who tormented his sleep.

Everything about her called to him. His need to dominate and control grew with every night's dream and the moment he was free there would be no stopping the beast.

FOUR

Kira startled awake the next morning when the sun slanted across her face from the open window, momentarily confused about her whereabouts and what had happened. As the fog of sleep faded away, she remembered checking into the motel.

She lay there, reliving her dream from the night before of the sensual and exciting man who would be her mate. Standing in front of her, his broad, muscular body had eclipsed her athletic frame, and he must have easily reached six-four.

Despite the tired expression she'd seen from her first vision, his gold and green eyes had sparked with energy and lust.

Her core squeezed as she remembered the intense feelings she had experienced while dreaming. In reality she wasn't sure how much longer she could last without him touching her.

I don't want it to be this way. There should be a choice—not force.

But the deep burn of need and desire wouldn't let go just because her brain said so.

"Lucas," she whispered aloud. Remembering him as the man she'd seen in her vision just before her car crash, she became convinced, more than ever, her powers were fucked.

With the heavy weight of responsibility pressing down on her shoulders, Kira rose to shower and dress before she hit the road again. She didn't want these feelings or the obligation that came with them. She already had a life she needed to get back to. One that wouldn't wait very long for her return.

While brushing her teeth, Kira reexamined her vision from the day before. The cell Lucas had been in seemed familiar. It reminded her of the many military cells she'd had to visit during interrogations.

She closed her eyes, summoning the exact image she'd seen. This is how the Tallan was supposed to be used. To help and discover, not hurt.

Once there, she glanced around, hoping to find clues that would give her a possible location. Part of her training in Marine Corps intelligence had required her to become familiar with most military bases and their brig facilities.

If he was in one of those, there was a damn good chance she'd seen it. She focused on a wall outside the cell door where the guard stood.

Noticing some faint writing, she struggled to zoom in on the spot. Navajo inscriptions, she realized. Kira struggled harder to remember why they seemed so familiar. There were military installations all over the country but not many were that close to Native American reservations.

Her brain sifted through the possibilities until it landed on an unlikely candidate.

"Fort Wingate."

Impossible. Officially, Fort Wingate had been closed for almost fifteen years, but it was occasionally used for missile testing, and, if she recalled correctly, portions of it leased by a civilian contractor that did some private work there for the government.

However, there were no day-to-day military operations and certainly no policing activities took place. That information would have been on her radar.

To Kira, this simply provided more damning evidence she really was losing her mind, and the rate of that loss was accelerating rapidly.

Sexual dream walking with her potential mate she understood, but envisioning the same man being held prisoner by the military and hidden away in a deserted facility was a little over the top, even for her.

She had to get a grip and figure out how to regain control. It wouldn't be long before the council hunted her down, and she didn't want to stand before them and plead her case.

Having a group of elders who knew little about her decide whether she was fit to live or die was unacceptable. She'd always found their system of determining when a clan member was a threat to the safety and secrets within rather archaic.

However, their rules were crystal clear in regards to the onset of the female mating call and they provided only one way to escape death. Find a secondary mate and perform the bonding ritual.

It was believed the mental connection between a bonded pair stopped the degradation of the Tallan and strengthened it instead. What wasn't fully understood was the long term effect of a non true mate exerting their will onto the other. But she'd seen first hand how her stepfather treated her mother and even if she couldn't prove it, she was certain he had found a way to take control.

She picked up her bag and slammed her belongings inside. Time to get back on the road, back to work and put as much distance between her and home as possible. Until she found an alternative solution she wouldn't make it easy for anyone to know exactly what she went through.

"I choose to live on my terms, and nobody else gets to say different." She spoke the words forcefully to her empty room, determined that saying them out loud made them stronger.

Now if she could just keep her mother out of her head…

CHAPTER FIVE

K ira knew better than to stop, but seeing the exit sign with the faded letters of Fort Wingate as she traveled along I40, made it impossible to resist.

Fortunately or unfortunately, depending on how she chose to look at it, the sun would set soon, giving her the cover of darkness to poke around if she needed it. Since she wasn't prepared to be caught trespassing on government property, she might.

But if she kept driving, she wouldn't know for sure and the doubts would plague her. Maybe it wouldn't hurt much to nose around enough to prove there's nothing here. Then she'd get back in her car and turn toward California once and for all and put all of this behind her.

At the unmanned front gate, a sign was posted that all visitors must report to Building 204 to register. Since her presence on any base would be questioned and verified, she opted to bypass check in and take the back service road that circled behind the facility where the brig would be located.

Explaining to clueless security why she needed to be here in the first place could prove a little awkward. And if they flagged her ID she'd have to answer to her commander as well. Even she wouldn't believe some lame ass story about a dream.

About a mile into the base, she spotted the sign indicating the Brig straight ahead. She slowed her car and slipped into a parking lot several buildings away. She'd approach the building on foot.

Just in case.

Before getting out of her car, she reached for the glove compartment to grab her Glock for extra firepower. With her hand on the knob she stopped. Carrying a non-military issue weapon on a military base was borrowing trouble she couldn't afford. Not to mention it screamed paranoid considering her military approved Sig was already strapped to her calf and concealed by her jeans.

Kira pushed open the car door and closed it gently, opening her senses as she moved. This close she should be able to pick something up. *If* someone was actually there.

She approached the back of the Brig and immediately noticed dusty, dark windows boarded up tight. Layers of grime gave the building a depressed and worn out look.

The facility appeared unused and abandoned, but she reached out anyway to try the rear door, and caught a glimpse of something from the corner of her eye.

Bending down, she picked up a cigarette butt that didn't look fifteen years old. She sniffed. Freshly burned tobacco.

Still doesn't mean anything.

Civilian employees probably walked by here everyday

while on their smoke break. Yet, the nagging sense of something off tingled across her scalp and a wave of unease crawled down her spine. Kira shook it off as best she could, checked the door, and confirmed it was indeed locked tight.

Determined to find conclusive evidence, she crept around the side of the building headed in the direction of the front door. As she neared the front of the structure, the hairs on the back of her neck stood on end, stopping her dead in her tracks.

Her senses were screaming now, something wasn't right here. She rubbed the base of her neck, rolling her head to loosen up the tight muscles. Her internal warnings were no joking matter and had saved her ass more than once.

She inched forward with a lot more caution and in-depth observation, while surveying the area around the building.

Still she saw and heard nothing, but her spidey sense was on high alert, and would not be ignored.

With that in mind, she proceeded to the front door.

CHAPTER
SIX

L ucas stiffened, his cat senses flaring to full alert. Someone new was approaching the area but he didn't recognize the scent. He sat up on his cot and sifted through all the extraneous shit between him and the new person until he could narrow in on only him. Wait. Not him.

Her. Female. Nervous. Strong. Not at all like his captors. The frenetic energy coming from her indicated she was more than human.

No way.

He closed his eyes and concentrated inward, testing for a telepathic link. When he found what he was looking for, his eyes popped open and the cougar rumbled in warning. It should not be that easy.

With little to lose at this point, he broached her security and wandered undetected through the stranger's mind and searched for answers. When he found nothing, he smiled. Sneaky. So if he couldn't read her thoughts on his own there was only one thing left to do.

Hoping to catch her off guard, he whispered into her mind. *Who are you and what are you doing here?*

Her shock at his voice in her head reverberated through his mind like a short stab with a needle as she frantically searched for a reason someone had so easily slipped inside her shields.

Her scattered thoughts froze seconds before she answered him.

I could ask you the same question but more importantly, get out of my head!

He laughed at her anger. Despite his questions about her presence, her voice soothed and calmed his nerves like a natural balm to his restless nature. She on the other hand was not calm. The sudden rise of her heartbeat alarmed him.

Whoever she was, he'd found a new opportunity to fuck with these people. So he played along.

Who are you and what do you want?

I'm Captain Akira MacDonald, U.S. Marines. I'm here to look into the suspected unauthorized use of this facility.

He shook his head in disappointment. Suspicious by nature and circumstance, he assumed they had sent a new female soldier in yet another lame attempt at getting him to cooperate.

Sorry, sweetheart, but sending you in here isn't going to change a thing. I'll tell you the same thing I told the last one. Although...

Her ability to communicate with him with her mind intrigued him enough to drag this out a few minutes more. There weren't a ton of paranormals with that ability, much less humans. Maybe there was more he could learn from her. So he continued.

I could use a good fuck.

Lucas faltered when her violent anger washed over him like a crashing wave. It threatened to choke him with its sheer strength. Maybe he didn't need to play with her after all. Bitter disappointment filled him before he backed down.

No use getting dragged down by someone new or wasting his time. He closed the mind link between them and lay back down with a satisfied smirk directed at the cameras that watched his every move day and night.

The bastards should know better by now.

CHAPTER
SEVEN

F ury surged through Kira.

She had come out of her way to find out if someone from the clans had been kidnapped, and this was the thanks she got?

She had half a mind to turn around and leave him here, show him just where his arrogance would get him. But if he ended up being what she thought he was, they had bigger problems than just the two of them.

She sighed as resignation overrode her anger. She'd have to get him out of here and open an investigation.

Ready to continue, the familiar tingle of magic erupted in Kira's ears as power surged through her mind, begging for release. When she finally succumbed to the call, her arms flung wide and the locked door burst open, taunting her to keep going.

In no mood to be discovered by a guard or suffer the consequences of using her power out in the open, she quickly ducked inside, and closed the door behind her.

Might have thought of that before you made all that racket

39

with the door. His voice whispered along the edge of her mind, unsettling her further.

Shut up. I need to concentrate.

A low chuckle sounded in response. *Don't expect my cooperation, sweetheart. I don't do nice.*

She took a deep breath to fortify her shields and kick him out of her head before proceeding.

Steady enough to continue, she attempted to get her bearings in the darkened room while she listened for any telltale signs of where he might be, as well as any guards. With an ego like his, she expected him to continue taunting her, but he surprised her when he said nothing.

"I came here to investigate," Kira whispered. No response. "Why are you being held? Have you committed a crime?" She waited and listened. "You can't stay here, it's too risky. I've got to take you back." Still she heard nothing. No breathing, no movement. No signs of life within the room.

Now he was just toying with her.

"Fine. Be that way." She crept forward, feeling her way in the darkened room. Her hand came in contact with the cold steel bars. She'd found a cell but had no idea which direction led to the door or where Lucas might be hiding within.

By instinct and touch, she located the cell door in minutes. She inhaled deeply. Entering the cell could be a big mistake, as exactly what waited inside for her remained a mystery. But a force stronger than her will compelled her forward. Again she concentrated on the lock, and her magic worked its way inside until the door slid open. Gripping the bars tightly, she started to move inside.

"Who are you and why are you here?" His menacing voice reached out to her, accompanied by a low growl that came from the opposite corner from where she stood.

"I already told you who I am and I'm not here to hurt you, only to find out information," she assured him. *Maybe this wasn't such a hot idea after all.*

"Darling, I'm not worried about YOU hurting me. I just don't feel like playing your game." His mocking tone grew stronger as he moved toward her.

When his big body moved through a sliver of light she had to bite back her gasp. Despite the snarl stamped across his face and the menacing muscles that flexed when he moved, the beautiful aura of a born leader nearly took her breath away.

Power radiated from him as he came closer, only to finally stop mere inches from her body. Though his closeness made her uncomfortable, she refused to back down and give him the satisfaction of thinking he scared her. To run from an Alpha, even one imprisoned in a cell, would weaken her position.

And if he gave chase...

With a brief thought to her weapon, she leaned forward and whispered in his ear, "I don't play games with strange men, so you can back the fuck off with the macho alpha male crap. You've been in my mind, so get real. You know the deal."

CHAPTER
EIGHT

Her warm sweet breath skittered across his skin, making him temporarily lose focus while also forgetting for an instant she was his enemy.

Instead, he fought an almost uncontrollable urge to take her to the ground, pin her arms to the cold concrete floor, and fuck her into a frenzy. The animal screamed in his head, wanting to be free and the raging hard-on pressing painfully against his zipper made it damned difficult to control the beast.

Her scent invading his nostrils had a spicy tang with a definite musk of arousal undertone, reminding him of his recent dreams and something else, something from a long time ago. He tried to get a good look at her, but even his enhanced vision couldn't see past her silly ball cap in the darkness.

While admiring her bitch-in-heat scent, he began to formulate a plan. She'd left the cell door unlocked with no guard in sight. And unlike him, she appeared to be having difficulty seeing in the dark, which made it ridiculously easy to grab her and use her as a hostage to get out of this godforsaken place.

Maybe too easy.

After allowing himself about fifteen seconds to decide a course of action, he flexed his forearms and his nails lengthened without a sound into lethally sharp weapons.

He grabbed her arms, spun her around and pulled her compact body flush up against his while placing his claws so precisely around her neck she couldn't move without him slicing into her flesh.

Instinctually, she fought back until his claw pierced her skin and drew a single drop of blood. The metallic scent filled the dank air, igniting his hunger. His vision hazed for a few brief seconds while he fought the instinct to dip down and tongue the essence from her neck. He could already see his teeth sliding into her neck to...

Dammit to hell. Get a fucking grip.

Lucas shook his head, forcing himself to focus. The animal obviously couldn't think straight. He was in control here.

She hissed through clenched teeth, "What the hell are you doing?"

He smiled into the darkness. "Sorry, hon, but it looks like you're my ticket out of here."

"Why? What have you done? Why are you being held here?"

The honey sweet smell of her fear mixed with the pungent odor of her anger permeated his senses. A momentary twinge of regret knotted in his stomach for having to involve her or hurt her, but this might be his only chance to escape.

"Nothing. In fact, the only thing I'm guilty of is trusting the wrong person. Let's hope I've learned my lesson not to trust a liar." And she'd certainly lied. He'd easily slid into her mind, but somehow she'd blocked him before he learned too much. Getting in, however, had been all too easy.

"Paranoid much? I don't lie."

"Whatever." Her honesty at this point didn't matter. He had one goal only. Gain his freedom and begin the hunt for his betrayer. "I only need to use you to get out of here, and then you can go back to wherever you came from."

Her body tensed in his arms, and he suspected she was planning to make a move against him.

"Look babe, if you just cooperate, this will be quick and painless." He paused, waiting for her response.

"I thought I was coming here to help you, asshole, but clearly you're not the man I thought you were. And don't ever call me babe again," she seethed through clenched teeth.

Her response made no sense, but he suspected it was simply another ploy to confuse him. His captors had tried every method of torture and coercion to break him, but they had to be feeling seriously desperate when they'd sent this woman.

"Let's go." He prodded her forward in short steps.

WHILE LUCAS WALKED her out of the cell, Kira nudged the Tallan to scan the nearby area for guards or any other people. He foolishly thought he was taking her against her will, but she knew the truth, and she'd play along to see where it led them... for a while.

Her neck throbbed from the small slice of his claw, and delaying their departure with hand-to-hand combat wasn't a smart tactical move at the moment. Truth be told, it wasn't just the danger that had her worried—being this close to her dream walker lit her body like gas on dried kindling. It was unsettling to say the least. Shaking her head, she refocused on the task at hand. Their connection would have to wait until they were in the free and clear.

For some strange reason, she found no one around. That simple fact had her internal warning blaring for attention. Something was off, but she couldn't take the time to analyze it now. They needed to get out before anyone returned, or worse, had time to attack. When they walked out the door of the facility, Kira noticed Lucas checking every detail around him for any sign of trouble. She'd bet anyone would be hard pressed to get anything by him.

Capturing him must have been a real bitch.

Despite her annoyance over his belief he could actually kidnap her, she couldn't help but admire his physique. The muscles of his torso rippled against her back with every lithe move he made. When he pulled her down in a crouch to stay hidden, he appeared every inch a predator waiting for his prey.

He turned to her, his mouth open to say something, and he froze. His eyes narrowed, dilated, and for an instant, time stood still as she watched the awareness dawn in his gaze. Those dark eyes pinned her in place and sparks shot through her at the uncontrollable lust coursing in her veins. She licked her lips and bit her bottom lip as he continued his intense perusal.

"How is this possible?" he asked. Kira closed her eyes and took a steady breath.

Obviously her suspicions had been correct. Snarl or no snarl, she recognized him. They'd walked through their dreams together, and from the telling way he devoured her with his gaze, he remembered every sensual minute.

Her face flushed with heat as the memories of what they'd done every night this week became all too real.

She parted her lips to respond, but he covered them with his own. Her world tilted. The reality of his possession was even more intoxicating than she'd dreamed. He thrust his tongue inside her mouth, and the fervent pressure of his lips against hers started an insistent throbbing between her legs.

Her dream man pulled her across his lap where his rapidly growing arousal pressed into her buttocks. Despite the potential for danger, she melted into his arms.

His hands roamed everywhere—along her spine, caressing her shoulders before finally sinking into her thick hair where he gripped a handful and jerked her off his lips. She yelped from the shock and pain of his action.

"What the hell is going on here?" Anger and lust shone equally from his soulful eyes.

Before Kira could respond, she was startled by an alternate image forming in her mind. "Someone's coming," she murmured. He dropped her from his lap, leaping away from her into a defensive crouch to listen.

She grabbed his hand and wordlessly tried to pull him toward her hidden car. He didn't budge.

"Look, pal, unless you want us both to get caught, something I definitely do NOT want, you need to trust me. I have a car nearby, but if we don't go now, the well armed bitch you're so fond of will be back and it'll be too late."

He stared at her for a moment, "I don't trust anyone but myself, so don't think for a second you can play me."

She dropped his hand, pulled her handgun from the ankle holster and took off for her car. She'd leave the bastard behind if that's the way he wanted to *play* it. More anger rolled from her in waves as she fled to the car.

CHAPTER
NINE

From a quarter of a mile away, in the corporate offices of a local construction company, Malcolm felt a tingling down his spine. It was a sure sign of trouble when the cat wanted out.

More tingling along his arms and the onslaught of excruciating pain racked his body. Sweat broke out across his torso. The all too familiar torment of needing to shift consumed him.

Except he couldn't shift.

His supposed family had set him on this course when they banished him and never looked back.

The energy build of his body trying to do what it had been designed to caused every muscle in his body to alternately cramp and convulse. Pain seared his blood as the darkness overrode his mind.

God dammit. What the hell had Lucas done now? Whatever it was it couldn't be good.

Grappling with the sensation of thousands of needles stabbing into him, he reached across the desk to phone the

51

guards. "What's happening with our subject?" His voice came out harsh, like broken glass in a blender.

"There seems to be a problem, sir."

Malcolm heard a slight tremble in the guard's voice when he answered, and some shouting in the background.

"While Lara was taking a quick break, your prisoner disappeared."

A white-hot rage erupted within him, the nature of his beast calling out to him from its prison as he savored the idea of killing the guard on the phone. A fresh wave of pain seized his gut when the animal hit the wall holding him in.

Malcolm took deep, calming breaths and temporarily banked down his angry desires. There would be time for that later. First he'd get the pain under control, then he'd take care of his useless guards.

"You and your team should begin reviewing the security tapes immediately, and send Lara to my office right now. I will deal with this breach myself."

These days he had a new outlet for this kind of situation.

Not a cure, but it usually at least made the torture bearable. Today it would be Lara and her ineptitude that would pay the price.

Damn that woman. Will she never fucking listen?

He'd warned her his brother was clever and cunning beyond her comprehension. She'd insisted her magic would hold him.

He slammed his fist on the desk. Good thing he'd anticipated something like this would happen and took proper measures in advance.

In the meantime, when that bitch got here, she'd have to beg for his forgiveness and pray he let her live.

Malcolm squeezed the edge of his desk, ignoring the wood shattering in his hands as more pain seized him. The beast would be free one way or another.

The fact he was already hard just from thinking about punishing her gave him hope. Releasing his rage on someone else might subdue the beast for a while.

He would have to beat her of course. Punish her for her continued failures, and if she could take it without begging for him to stop, he'd reward her by stuffing his cock in her wanting mouth. Or she could take it another way. He might let her choose this time.

His body tingled with the anticipation of pleasure those images conjured as he began taking his belt off.

Whatever it took to regain control...

CHAPTER
TEN

Lucas was in shock. He couldn't believe the woman from his dreams sat beside him. Now, as they traveled down the highway, he struggled to figure out what the hell to do next. Her hands gripped the steering wheel a little too tight, and her mouth pursed in a thin, straight line. Her silence left him unsure whether she was frightened or pissed. He scented a little of both, but couldn't tell which emotion controlled her at the moment.

"Where to?" she asked.

Back at the base, he'd managed to snag her shirt as she ran and wrestle her to the ground just before she reached her car. Their brief tussle ended with a carefully placed claw to remind her who was in charge, then her handing over her gun, which now sat on the floorboard as far away from her as possible. That she carried such a sweet weapon impressed and intrigued him.

"Keep going east on 40 and I'll let you know." He stretched and shifted his legs, trying to get comfortable in her tiny car. Who in their right mind spent good money on a vehicle with no legroom?

"Are you going to make me drive all the way back to North Carolina?"

He opened his eyes and gazed at her curiously. *Fuck.* She knew where he was from? What else did she know? And what kind of game was she trying to play now?

Giving up on comfort, he straightened to an upright position on the seat and leaned forward.

"Where do you think I'm leading you to?" he demanded. It was all he could do to concentrate on his plan when it was her lips that captured much of his attention.

Plump and slightly parted, she alternately licked them or bit at them with her teeth. Both actions made his dick ache. He was definitely on a slippery slope.

The ache to kiss her again overwhelmed him, made the need to discover exactly how urgent and real his dreams had been. He leaned over and whispered in her ear, "What do you want from *me*, Akira MacDonald of the U.S. Marines?"

Her shuddering response brought a smile to his face. Nice to see he didn't suffer alone and the attraction went both ways.

"What makes you think I want anything? Well, other than my freedom, of course."

"There is that..." He relaxed back in the seat, putting some space between them, and began formulating a plan to get back home. He was far enough away from his captors he could likely ditch her and get there on his own, but something about her nagged at him, something suspiciously like...nah, that couldn't be.

His gaze wandered back to her, drinking in her appearance through hooded eyes. He admired the strong lines of her face, the petite nose above full, lush lips he already knew were kissable. It made him wonder.

Why this woman and why now? Why would he have dreams about a stranger who wanted to not only use him, but also likely kill him?

He could close his eyes and will her image out of his head, but there was nothing to save him from her scent. The fresh and sweet smell wouldn't leave him. This was one of those rare times he cursed his abilities.

So instead he watched her.

Her breasts rose gently with each breath she took, and he wondered if her nipples would pucker and swell as he'd dreamt. Or turn instantly hard when he kissed her?

Damn, his agony worsened as his cock tightened beyond anything he had experienced before. No, he wouldn't be letting her go yet. Not until he tasted more of her, savoring every inch as he went. Then he'd slide inside her and feel her slick heat tighten around him.

Yeah, he was a bastard. But he needed her and, one way or another, it would be soon.

CHAPTER
ELEVEN

Kira felt his gaze on her body, studying her as surely as if his hands roamed her curves. She didn't want to admit just how hot she burned for him, but with the nagging thought of going mad without him touching her, she couldn't exactly deny it.

Heat burned inside her while she struggled to think of something else. How could she feel this way about an arrogant jerk that made no secret of both his dislike for as well as his willingness to fuck her?

She tried to nudge herself into his thoughts, but his new barriers against her were impossible to penetrate.

Who the hell is he? And why the hell can't I get in?

Despite the tension between them, her stomach rumbled like a starved bear.

"Akira, when was the last time you ate something? You're growling at me."

"It's just Kira. Nobody calls me Akira. And yes, I'm famished," she mumbled.

For more than just food, though.

"We should stop soon. You've been driving for hours. There's an exit coming up with restaurants and hotels. We'll stop there for the night."

Her stomach flipped. A hotel? Since he was still under the misguided impression he'd kidnapped her, he'd probably insist on only one room.

Wicked thoughts of being alone with her dream man filled her head, all of which featured one or both of them naked. If he took off any more clothes, no way could she be held responsible for what happened.

Can I possibly resist him? Do I want to?

"Sounds like a plan. I'm definitely ready for a break and some food."

She pulled the car on the exit ramp and followed the signs to a Denny's, which happened to be the closest stop. She had to get out of the car as quickly as possible. She needed space between them before she did something she knew she'd regret.

Once parked, she climbed from the car and raised to her tiptoes to stretch and move her stiffened limbs. The long ride cramped her muscles and it felt so good to move.

Midstretch, she glanced at Lucas and found him staring at her. Her skin tingled under the examination and a steady throb quickened her sex. She doubted even space would keep them apart at this rate.

"You ready?" His question came out gruff and unsteady.

Kira bit her top lip to hold back the smile at his surliness. *Guess Mr. Macho Alpha man has a weakness, too.* She nodded and headed for the entrance. Now she only had to decide whether she could risk letting him get any closer.

At the door she stopped to let a family of four pass by. His arm brushed against her back, sending a sudden streak of pleasure zipping through her. She sucked in a sharp, deep breath as her skin tingled and heated.

Oh Goddess, this is going to be a long night.

CHAPTER
TWELVE

Lucas studied Kira's backside as she followed the waitress to a table. He couldn't ever remember seeing a finer ass wrapped in tight denim. Her skirt rose up when she slid sideways into the booth first, giving him a quick flash of tempting black lace.

Forcing himself to turn away from her bare thighs, he took the spot across from her and caught her watching him with interest. She gave him a small smile, and for one brief unguarded moment he saw a different woman.

Not the one of his dreams or the trained soldier, but instead a softer side he longed to discover. His gaze focused on her soft, pink lips and the straight, white teeth nibbling on the corner of her lower lip every time she sucked it in.

He picked up his menu and tried to concentrate on the words printed in front of him and not the lush mouth he wanted to devour.

"What can I get you?" The waitress looked between them expectantly.

"I'll take the French toast platter with three slices of extra bacon and some hot chocolate with extra whipped cream, please."

He looked at her in surprise.

"What? I'm hungry," she said.

Shaking his head, he laughed, charmed beyond belief by the smile she kept flashing. After he ordered his own hearty breakfast, he waited until the waitress walked off before he lifted his eyes to Kira again.

He turned her way and their gazes locked onto each other. This time there was no cute smile. Instead, a look of pure heat and curiosity. Her tongue darted out to lick her bottom lip and the urge to swipe his own tongue across her slammed into him. The simple fact of her proximity threatened his ability to stay aloof. His cock twitched in his pants and he gripped the edge of the seat he sat on to keep from dragging her across the table and kissing her senseless.

"Why were you being held captive?"

She didn't mince words when she wanted to know something. A trait he had a hard time not admiring.

"You really don't know? Seriously, don't they tell you people anything?"

She opened her mouth to say something and must have changed her mind as she shut it and remained quiet.

Her expression changed, closed down, and he felt bad for being a smart ass, even though he had no reason to feel that way.

"Why don't we talk about something else?" Something safe maybe.

"Like what?"

Her question brought to mind every dirty thought he'd

tried to push away. What would she say if he told her all he really wanted to do right now was lay her out in front of him, spread her legs wide, and feast on her instead of the food they'd ordered?

He imagined she tasted even sweeter than the scent of her arousal that continued to torment him. He shifted uncomfortably on the bench, grateful for the cover of the table.

"What about the—"

"Here ya go, sugar. Your French toast and hot chocolate, and your omelet and coffee." The waitress set the plates of steaming food in front of them and flashed an extra friendly smile to him. "Can I get you anything else?"

She didn't even bother to look at Kira this time, but he did. "Need anything else?" he asked her.

She shook her head, casting her eyes on her food.

"I guess we're all set then." With his thoughts consumed by the urge to touch her, he reached across the table and covered Kira's hand with his own, dismissing the waitress. When their skin touched, he forgot about everything except her. Her heat reignited his barely cooled lust until his body burned to claim her.

"Lucas, I—I need my hand to eat." Her whisper caught his attention and he realized he'd been holding her too tight. He loosened his fingers and pulled back. She appeared calm, but he heard the acceleration of her heartbeat as she picked up her fork and worked at cutting her breakfast into small bites.

Her movements mesmerized him. When she lifted her fork to sample the food, her mouth formed the perfect O as she took it all inside and clamped her lips around the utensil. Withdrawing the fork, she left behind a dusting of powdered sugar and a few drops of sugary syrup on her bottom lip. All of which he wanted to lick clean for her.

Blood roared in his ears as she repeated the process over and over. Since he couldn't take his eyes off of her, his own food laid untouched.

"You not hungry anymore?" she asked.

"Not really."

"That's too bad. It's really good." She licked the last of the sugar from her lips, picked up her cocoa and lapped at the whipped cream. The damn woman tempted him to his core, which here in public was not the best of ideas.

A low growl sounded from his throat before he could think to stop it, and her gaze shot to his. Questioning him.

"It's time to go." He couldn't hide the deep rumble of need in his voice.

"Why? What's wrong?" Lucas flipped through his wallet, grabbed some bills and threw more than enough on the table to cover their meal and tip before grabbing her hand and dragging her from the restaurant.

"But I wasn't finished!"

He simply growled in response.

When they stepped outside the diner, Lucas dragged the cool night air into his lungs searching for his control. Only two things could happen right now: shift or fuck. Neither option seemed viable until he noticed the woods across the road. The urge to change and go for a run crawled up his body, taking over and making his skin too tight. He inhaled the clean scent of pine trees, the musky earth and various small wildlife.

He yearned to run free again. To be at home in his

mountains where he didn't have to watch his back with every move and worry as much about exposing secrets. It had been too long. He crossed the street and headed for the cover of trees and shrubs, away from the busy restaurant and cars.

Without considering the consequences, he allowed the familiar prickling of his skin as the changes rushed across him, fur quickly covering his arms. It had been too long.

A branch snapping behind him reverberated through him like a gunshot, startling him back from his selfish thoughts as he realized what he'd almost done. He'd been about to change in front of the enemy. The very thing he'd fought against all these weeks. After taking a few moments to regain control over his traitorous body, he turned to face Kira.

Her eyes were wide and full of questions, yet she said nothing. Did she already know what he was or would it shock her to see him turn into a wild beast?

While carefully watching her responses, Lucas motioned behind him. "There's a pathway across the street. Do you feel up to a short walk in the woods?" Surprisingly, he didn't smell fear on her at his request, and her heartbeat had only increased a few beats per minute.

"Yes, please. I'm not ready to get back into that car again or go inside anytime soon. I'd love some fresh air. And then I'd like to know what the hell happened back there."

He snorted. "You like the woods?"

"Grew up in them. There were miles and miles of unspoiled beauty back home I could roam and play in.

Loved getting lost so much I took to disappearing for days. Drove my mother berserk."

His chest clenched at the genuine smile of happiness her memory created. "Where at?" Kira's smile faded and he realized he'd pushed too far.

"A long way from here."

He waited for her to reveal more, but her face remained closed. Stepping forward, he gripped her hand and led the way deep into the woods. The instant he touched her a connection sizzled between them, sending heat throughout his limbs.

His body reacted, growing taut with desire. Once again the urge to take her in every possible way consumed his thoughts. Time or place no longer mattered. Pure, primal need for her coursed through him.

What is wrong with me? Since when can't I control myself with a woman? Especially this one.

He knew she'd been sent to draw information from him. Just how far would she go to succeed in her mission?

She was obviously telepathic, what other abilities did she possess? He wanted to focus on the anger those thoughts created, but the animal clawed into his gut to get out when he did. Something he couldn't allow.

So he'd focus on the woman—the sassy woman he'd glimpsed in the diner, the one who spoke of spending her childhood in the woods. Kira abruptly stopped and whirled around to face him.

"You're wrong about me you know," she blurted out. "I'm not who you think I am." Despite the nervous way she bounced from foot to foot, her eyes blazed, daring him to challenge her.

Her lush mouth mesmerized him. Lucas couldn't focus on what she'd been saying over the roaring rush of blood in his sensitive ears.

Her tongue darted out to moisten her lips. The memory of that tongue pressed to his skin flashed through his mind and his entire body tightened further. He fought the urges until lust seeped from every pore and he snapped.

He grabbed her shoulders and crushed her against his chest.

"What—" Before she could finish, he took her mouth with a rough, demanding kiss. He thrust his tongue past her teeth and devoured her taste, reveling in the silken warmth. Stroking into her heat, he gave up fighting the need any longer.

His beast wouldn't be denied. Lucas wanted her more than his next breath and, by damn, he was going to have her.

Now.

CHAPTER
THIRTEEN

Kira's brain scrambled as the hardness of his chest pushed up against her breasts and his heat burned straight through to her skin. She wanted him buried deep inside her.

Now.

She grabbed his hair and tried to pull him closer as their kiss became frantic. He bit at her lips then stroked her with his rough, textured tongue.

She thought about trying to stop—this was too soon, too fast—but when Lucas lifted her skirt and ripped her panties away from her trembling body, she lost the last of her doubts.

"The scent of your arousal is enough to make a grown man weep and beg. Tell me to stop. Just say anything to make me believe your pussy isn't dripping wet with need."

She trembled in his arms. Words couldn't form so she shook her head instead. Here with the heat of his body pressed against her, a wicked lust visible on his face, she could forget about the future. She needed this pleasure, and when it was over she'd exorcise him from her dreams and be done with him.

Helplessly, with no control to stop herself, she arched her back, urging him on.

"This time it's not a dream. Are you ready for that?" He moved closer, his teeth grazing her jaw line in the direction of her ear. "You smell wild and sweet, like the mountain forest after a soaking rain. I love the rain."

He sank two fingers inside her and started a slow agonizing pumping pumping rhythm, driving her mad.

"Akira, baby, I ache for this. I've tried to resist but I just can't. I've suffered with the scent of your need filling my head for too long. It's driving me crazy, but I won't force you. If you want this you have to tell me."

He hesitated, obviously waiting for her response. Those dark, demanding eyes looked deep inside her, demanding her answer.

Hunger raged between then and, when she didn't answer right away, he thumbed her clit. Her body jolted, arching into his hand, striving to find the hard pressure that would satisfy the unrelenting ache.

He needed to quit toying with her and get on with it already.

Her breath caught in her throat when his fingers hit the sweet spot inside her. "Please, Lucas. Please." She couldn't fight, not the pleasure, not him. It consumed her.

"Please what, baby?" He delved further, scissoring to stretch and fill her. They both breathed harder, their pants echoing around them.

On a desperate whimper and breathless cry, she screamed out, "Just fuck me already, ok? Is that what you wanted?"

"Fuck yeah, baby."

"Fine. Then do it. Please."

With her words, the animal she suspected inside him broke free. He reached down and, in one smooth jerk, ripped her shirt and bra open to bare her breasts and belly to his gaze, then pinched one of her already puckered nipples.

She shrieked, excited by his every touch and reaction.

Common sense fled and she found herself on the verge of a pleasure precipice, and she was afraid he knew it. As he alternately pulled and sucked at her nipples, she began fumbling with his pants in an effort to get him free.

After a tense, struggling moment, his heavy erection sprang loose. She immediately grasped him, marveling at the size as well as the contrasting sensation of baby soft skin covering hard steel.

And as long and thick as he was, she understood why he was readying her with his fingers. He wanted to fit inside without hurting her.

She looked down, anxious to see more. The ruddy color of his shaft contrasted against his lightly furred, tanned abs. Of course the man had a six pack.

A bead of moisture formed at his tip, catching her eye and making her long to take him in her mouth. Then maybe she could drive him as crazy as he drove her.

At her touch, Lucas seemed to lose all of his control. Low, loud growls emerged from his throat. He pushed her back against a tree, pushing her skirt farther out of the way, lifting her legs around his waist, and plunged deep inside her with one urgent stroke.

Oh, God.

Lucas covered her mouth with his own, muffling her screams and moans, while not moving as her body adjusted to his size. After a moment of stillness, she wrenched her mouth free, gasping for air.

"What are you waiting for?" she cried.

"You're tighter than I expected, and I don't want to hurt you."

"Screw that." She'd crawl out of her skin if he didn't move. "Hard. Fast. Move now."

That was all the encouragement he needed. He struggled against straining muscle to pull his entire length back out but her body was too eager and his cock so thick. The pleasure ripples alone were almost more than she could bear. Already the tease of release tugged at her core, sizzling across her nerves.

"Dammit. So fucking tight. You're going to make me come too fast."

She wiggled against him wildly when everything exploded, little splinters of light and sensation rushing through her, leaving her breathless. Her nails clawed at his back, sinking deep into his flesh. Ecstasy burned straight through her, filling her, mending pieces of her soul she hadn't even realized were broken.

She rode out the orgasm, wrenching every last drop of pleasure. His body tensed, rigid and stiff underneath her arms and legs where she was wrapped around him seconds before he bellowed out his own release.

Exhausted and satisfied, she slumped forward against his chest and listened as his wild heartbeat began to slow and finally beat nice and steady.

As the orgasm induced fog in her brain began to fade, a not so tiny piece of her wanted to admit she did indeed need her mate. A fact she didn't know how to handle at the moment.

She squeezed her eyes shut tight.

What am I going to do?

If she hadn't been sure before, the tingling and tightening of her birthmark was a dead give away. Until now she'd ignored the sacred mating mark she'd been born with, unwilling to believe she had no control over her fate.

Not to mention it signified a cross species mating that was as far as she knew, still strictly forbidden by his clan.

God, she didn't have time to deal with this in her life right now, let alone how he must feel.

Then there was the annoying fact that without him she'd die. Something he wouldn't know unless she told him. She exhaled into his chest. Some secrets were better left kept.

As far as he was concerned, she was just the enemy he wanted to fuck. She doubted he thought anything beyond a wham-bam-thank-you-ma'am.

Yet, he'd taken her with a force and need far more complex than a simple "once is all I need." Or so she wanted to believe.

What would he think when he found out who and what she was to him? How could he not already know? Her mind was overloading with too much random information. None of which made any sense.

She pushed away her desperate fears and straightened her spine, remembering who she was and her own abilities. Not only could she handle this, but much more if she had to. She refused to believe she needed a man to complete her. There had to be another way.

Lucas withdrew from her and lowered her to her feet, taking an awkward step away from her. "Uhm, it looks like I ruined your clothes."

He avoided her eyes as he spoke, and she'd bet her last dollar he wanted nothing more than to get away from her. She couldn't blame him. Being alone right now would be a helluva a lot better than this awkward "what now" feeling.

She had to fight the urge to jump when he turned his fiery gold gaze her way. His change in eye color unnerved her. His pupils had dilated enlarging the golden centers and leaving very little of the dominant green hue she'd seen before.

Add to that the fact he didn't look too worried. In fact he looked smug.

"It's okay. My skirt is fine, and I'll just tie my shirt together until we get to the car. I have plenty of clothes in the trunk to change into." She did her best to stand there, head held high, as if what was happening between them was no big deal. Except inside her stomach churned.

He watched her every move as she gathered herself together. She couldn't tell whether he wanted to run or go again and the uncertainty of her emotions and his scrutiny left her uneasy. She curled her trembling fingers into the fabric of her shirt, determined to hide her weakness from him.

"Can we go back now? I want to get cleaned up?" Exhaustion began to set in as she pressed a hand over her eyes as a nagging pain settled in her head.

"Yeah, let's see about finding a motel for the night, so we both can shower and get some sleep."

CHAPTER
FOURTEEN

Kira savored the steamy water rolling over her body. She winced when the heat stung some of the scratches from the tree. The momentary ease had been worth each and every scratch and scrape.

Even now she couldn't get the image of Lucas taking her so frantically and roughly out of her mind. The fierce desire that drove him still hammered through her veins.

She still felt his lips pressed against her burning skin, tasting and taking whatever he wanted. It had happened as if he *needed* her, much more than simple want.

Yeah right.

Asking him to sacrifice his life to mate with her and save her from the madness was out of the question. Only, how much longer would she be able to control it?

The nagging headache from the woods had gone full blown and if she didn't get it back under control something bad was bound to happen. Her episodes of mania were getting worse—and more frequent.

Leaning forward, she pressed her forehead against the

cool tiles and shut her eyes, reliving every moment of the delicious and incredible episode they had shared despite her need to focus on something safer.

With the memory of his breath at her ear and his hand on her naked breast, sudden pain pierced her head and robbed her of breath.

Kira pressed her hands to her temples. The memories from the woods were quickly twisting and turning into something she no longer recognized. Something not real she hoped. It was already impossible to tell. Her mind and her memories were no longer her own.

No. Not now. Please not now.

As Lucas pumped into her, he taunted, "Is this what you wanted, whore? Planning to fuck me until I don't care what I tell you about my family?" His anger was clear as he slammed into her again.

"No, you don't understand. I am like you, but different." She pleaded for his acceptance, though she knew from the anger in his eyes he would never give it.

"You are a liar and a whore. Trading your body for information." He grunted as he fucked her faster. "I hate women like you."

His words were harsh and rough. Her own protective instincts rushed forward, filling her body with rage. She pounded on his chest, trying to make him stop, but her body was pinned tight with no way to escape.

"You wanted to see the beast, right? That's what all of this is about isn't? Then lift your head and take a good long look. The *monster is here and he's going to take from you whatever he wants.*

He laughed at her, the tone so mocking she couldn't breathe....

SHE FELL to her knees in the shower as the water pounded against her back.

No. No. No! Not the truth. Not the truth. Not how it happened.

Her fist slammed into the tiled wall over and over in frustration, splitting the skin of several knuckles. This had to stop.

As she stayed there sobbing into the water while clutching her arms around her waist, the fog in her brain began to clear and her real memories started to return.

Only then did she realize how much her condition had worsened in the last twenty-four hours. Her ability to control it had slipped.

In that moment in the woods, Lucas had loved her like no other man could. The way a true mate would. And now her mind wanted to play stupid tricks on her again, feeding her fear of the bonding ritual.

No way would she succumb to the anger and hatred eating away at her mind. She could control it. She knew right from wrong dammit.

But there had to be a way to fight the change without him. A mating between their clans would never be allowed. Their councils would banish them both, a sacrifice she wasn't prepared to ask of someone she barely knew.

For a mating to work, there had to be love. Not a forced ritual.

When the water ran cold, she struggled to stand on shaky legs and turned off the shower.

Enough bullshit. She would find a way out of this on her own.

FIFTEEN

Lucas heard the water shut off. Kira had been hiding in the bathroom since they'd arrived at a nearby motel. It was apparent she couldn't wait to erase him from her body.

He sighed. Probably for the best considering what happened in the woods had shaken him to his very core. He didn't understand how things had gotten out of his control, but it was time to get it back.

Was this all part of her plan? For the first time since he'd grabbed her, Lucas began to think kidnapping Kira was a really bad idea. The sooner he got away from her the better.

He hesitated. For some reason the thought of not being able to touch her again caused his stomach to cramp.

Yeah, definitely time to get rid of her.

And despite what happened, she couldn't be trusted.

In the morning, he'd leave her and make his way home alone. She was a big girl and could find her own way back to wherever the hell she came from.

He rubbed his face between his hands, wearier than ever. He needed to get some rest in order to think straight. The thoughts and urges running through his head made it impossible to lay still.

He stood up to pace instead. Instinct told him big changes were happening around him and he'd learned long ago to trust that kind of gut reaction. It was Kira. From the moment she'd walked into his dreams, everything had shifted and he'd become obsessed.

Even now the thought of her rubbing her lush body with a towel at this very moment was enough to make his mouth go dry and his mind and body fill with lust.

Everything earlier had been rushed, now he wanted a chance to explore, to sample. Her pale skin would be moist and succulent, flushed from the heat of the water. His cock stirred again.

Part of him was afraid for her to come out because he knew she would be irresistible. He stared at the bed and imagined her lying underneath him, begging for more. He would savor every minute of pleasure he could give her and she would reward him with those soft eyes and little cries of need.

He shook his head in disgust. *Get a fucking grip, man*. Hell, if he didn't pull himself together he'd find himself at her mercy or worse.

As the door opened and Kira stepped out of the bathroom, he froze in midstep.

"What?" she asked.

The sight of her in the simple green tank top with USMC stamped across the chest and running shorts was enough to make him lose it.

Memories of a similar outfit from a dream sent cold chills racing up and down his spine. The material barely covered her ass, and her tanned legs went on forever. Fuck, he wanted her now even more than in the woods—if that was possible.

"Nothing. I was just going over what I need to do tomorrow." He walked to the window and took some deep, and hopefully calming breaths, attempting to slow his racing heart.

His hand pushed on his crotch, desperate to find a comfortable spot in his pants. The beast pressed at his skin, tempting him. The animal inside wanted her as much as he did, making the situation even more confusing. Why did he care so much?

"Are we going to Dragon Tail?"

He froze. What the hell did she just say? How could she know? The thought that his home and haven had been compromised caused searing pain deep in his chest. It was his duty to protect them at all costs and yet he had managed to lead them to the front fucking door. Fresh rage beat down the arousal.

"What do you know about that?" He turned and slowly stalked her, waiting for an answer.

Her eyes glinted as she spoke, "It's our home."

The mere thought of her exposing his family had the fur rippling across his skin. He wanted to change, needed to change. If he did, he wasn't sure he could prevent himself from hurting her. He would do anything to keep his secrets, even resort to violence. Especially violence. It was his specialty.

"Wait, what did you say?" He couldn't have heard her

right. "Did you say our—" Lucas stopped mid-sentence when his nose tingled, his heightened senses picking up the scent of danger and a whole lot of firepower.

Gunpowder. His head pivoted toward the window as a rumbling growl sounded deep within, an instinctive response to intruders.

He heard them talking and smelled their approach. "What have you done?" he gritted out. When she tried to say something, he roughly covered her mouth and jerked her against him. "Quiet, woman. I have to think." He scented her anger and impatience radiating from her skin but, thankfully, she stayed quiet. He was going to have to use her again to get free and probably keep her for a while longer, despite his gut telling him what a mistake that would be.

After ravishing her in the woods, something he couldn't explain had happened. He had softened toward her. Allowed a weakness to slip inside that could go very wrong for him and his kind.

Now he just wanted to escape her lure, and all along she'd been using his lust to slow him down and plan his recapture.

A fatal mistake on her part. After they escaped again, he would find a way to make her pay and enjoy every minute of it.

He let the red rage of anger simmer closer to the surface, the beast within fighting for control. Obviously he'd taken the "keep your enemies close" a little too far with her.

CHAPTER
SIXTEEN

K ira took a deep breath and reached for the Tallan, hoping that magical connection that let her see things others couldn't would give her some insight as to what was happening. His instincts were sending out crazy alarm bells and she needed to see what they were up against outside.

After a few relaxing breaths and a forced concentration on her part, her vision cleared, revealing the men out front who planned to attack them. "Lucas, there are only four men out there. If we leave right this second and head down the south stairwell, I think we can avoid them or at the very least get a short head start."

When he didn't respond, she glanced over her shoulder to see if he was still there. His eyes were gold, glowing slits, just like a cat's. She'd seen those very eyes in a nightmare recently—or maybe a dream.

He'd started to change outside the diner and she hadn't even been surprised. Somehow she knew him, and not just from her dreams. Everything about him seemed natural to her.

Now his anger shimmered off of him, creating a sense of dread around them. His tight stance indicated a predator about to spring. Even without the Tallan she saw his struggle to hold back the beast. What would happen if he changed now? Would he hurt her?

She reached up and stroked his cheek, keeping eye contact the entire time, praying he wouldn't bite her with those sharp canines of his.

After a few long, tension filled minutes, his eyes faded to a softer gold and green again, maybe regaining a semblance of control. At least she hoped. He stepped closer to her, hissing in her ear,

"Be careful how you handle this, Akira. If you don't want anyone out there to die, then I suggest you do what I say."

Despite the wave of sheer terror rolling over her at the menacing tone of his voice, her own proclivity to violence increased, really pissing her off.

She rolled her eyes at him. "I'm getting sick and tired of you treating me like an idiot. I came to help you and, damn it, that's what I'm going to do."

He snorted, and she shot him a hard glare, daring the smug son of a bitch to laugh at her.

"Babe, you have no idea what you've gotten yourself into. Unfortunately, we don't have time for a sit down chat for me to explain. It's time to go."

Without words, she grabbed her backpack and slung it on her back. She reached for her shoes and headed for the door, not bothering to look behind to see if he followed her. At the moment, she didn't care. His trust issues grated on her nerves and she needed out of this situation. The sooner the better.

As she started down the stairs she felt the now familiar push of him at her mind. "Kira, wait."

Giving him a small break, she answered without even looking back, "We don't have time to chat. They're moving in."

"Where are they now?"

She hesitated. "Right outside our room, preparing to throw a nerve gas can." As soon as she spoke, breaking glass sounded from the direction of their room, causing them both to take off in a dead run. In seconds the soldiers would ascertain they'd fled, giving them precious little time to get away.

"I think we can just make it to the car." She picked up speed, daring him to keep up. They rushed down the stairs and sprinted across the parking lot.

A few yards from the car, Kira came to an abrupt halt, causing him to crash into her back. She tumbled forward but Lucas snaked his arm around her waist and caught her before she hit the ground.

"What the hell are you stopping for?"

"Something isn't right. I can feel it, but I don't see it." She twisted in his arms, breaking his hold. "We're missing something important here. Almost feels like..." She began frantically looking around for a clue or a sign of what "it" was.

As Kira tried to find out what pulled at her, the pounding of boots scrambling down the stairs behind them grew louder.

Lucas jumped in the car and started up the engine to leave. "Get in the damn car now!"

"I can't. Something's really wrong here and I'm—I'm trapped."

"Yeah, I'm about to get captured again, something I'm completely against. Are you planning to watch the torture this time?" The waves of his anger pushed at her, trying to force her to do what he wanted. But something else already had her in its grip, keeping her riveted to the spot from an unseen source until she figured it out.

She turned back to the motel, searching for signs or a clue, but all she found were four pissed off men emerging from the stairwell and running towards her. They carried some very angry looking weapons now aimed directly at her chest.

"Stop right there."

She held up her hands in a gesture of surrender. When the first man stepped forward, a menacing growl sounded behind her. Oh boy, if Lucas was losing it this was going to get messy.

When the man in front of her peered over her shoulder, the sight must have frightened him. He took several steps back, keeping his eyes on Lucas instead of her.

From the corner of her eye, she watched Lucas jump from the car, his body changing as he moved. Bones crunched and shifted, teeth elongated, clothes ripped. Claws on his hands and feet sprang free, and dark fur rippled along his skin. He grabbed her with his hands, which were all too quickly becoming paws, pushed her across the passenger's seat, and roared at her, "Drive!"

Holy shit, drive the damn car, Kira.

Thanks to the adrenaline coursing through her, along with years of military training, she gunned the screaming car out of the parking lot like a demon bat out of hell as the men behind them opened fire.

Bullets bit into the metal of the car as she swerved back and forth and focused on escape. As Kira rounded out of sight of the motel, one last shot hit the back window, shattering the glass.

Keep going, Kira. Don't hesitate. Lucas' voice in her head was both urgent and strangely comforting as they cleared the area with no sign of a tail.

Seeing Lucas go through his change from a maybe six and a half foot, heavily muscled man to a sleek, powerful looking cougar had been more than a little scary.

She'd grown up hearing the stories about his clan, but neither she nor anyone she knew had ever actually seen one in their shifted form.

They were known as solitary, independent creatures who didn't like to associate with other clans and usually spent great periods of time away from their own families. Especially the males.

After all these years she'd never quite believed until she witnessed it with her own eyes.

Minutes clicked by as she contemplated what to do next. He sat in the seat behind her but she was afraid to look. How would she feel looking into the eyes of her lover in the face of a big cat? She tried nudging his mind to hear his thoughts, but he was locked up tight. *Now what?*

Taking in a deep breath, she lifted her gaze and glanced in the rear view mirror to see nothing. She jerked around in momentary panic to find him lying across the back seat with his head resting on his paws and his eyes closed.

A soft gasp escaped her. He wasn't just a cougar, he was *the* cougar. The legendary black cougar she'd heard stories of, the one everyone said didn't exist, the one she'd encountered one day as a child...the one she'd spent years searching for. Even after she'd eventually convinced herself had to have been a dream.

A dream. It all made so much more sense now.

Well hell, she'd have to find a safe place for them to stop so they could finally have a talk. She needed some answers and it was way past time for him to know the truth, and damned if she didn't want to admire his new shape. Her curiosity was killing her.

Focusing on the road once again, she began plotting where to stop and what she'd say to him. He wasn't going to like the truth. If he even believed her. The truth always seemed stranger than fiction.

Thinking about the narrow escape, she remembered the strange sensations she'd encountered as she'd approached the car. And why weren't they being pursued? Whoever they were had gone to great lengths to find them to just suddenly let them go.

I'm missing something critical here, I just know it. Now she had to figure it out before it was too late.

CHAPTER
SEVENTEEN

The car came to an unexpected stop, making Lucas sit up and look around. He must have finally dozed off because it had turned dark outside. No problem for him now because of his superior night vision when in cat form.

Kira had parked them at the far side of a rest area but had pulled the car as close to the cover of woods as she could. A fat moon shone through the trees, enticing him.

He turned and gazed at Kira. She just sat there with her head on the steering wheel, not moving. Was she scared of him? He didn't smell fear. It was more like—he lifted his head and sniffed—anxiety or anticipation. He couldn't be sure.

He debated shifting back to human form but it had been too long since he'd done this and he wanted—no, needed—to get out and run and be alone for at least a short while.

He pushed his upper body between the two front seats and nudged his nose against her hand and purred to get her attention. She jumped at his touch, turning to finally face him. For one quick moment he spotted an unexpected emotion—sadness—in her eyes before she went blank.

"Do you need help getting out or something?"

Her voice carried a rich and husky tone, the kind of sound that skittered right down his spine, causing a strong shudder. *Yes, I need to be alone for a while.* He gentled his own tone in her mind, trying to gauge her openness to him. *Can I trust you to be here when I get back?*

Exhaling what he guessed to be a heaping sigh of frustration, she simply said, "Yes."

Kira leaned across the seat and opened the door and turned back to stare out the windshield. Whatever thoughts ran through her mind, she likely needed some time to deal with them as much as he did.

He bounded out the open door and into the woods faster than the normal human eye would notice. If he'd caught the attention of anyone, all they'd recall was a black blur they couldn't identify.

After hours of running, hunting and thinking, he couldn't find a way to stop his body from craving her. Or the burn of need driving him mad. He had left her alone in the car because the animal needed freedom. But what he'd really needed was to get away from her to clear his system, exhaust his body with a run, and get his mind to a more lucid state that didn't include thoughts of her tight body squeezing his cock every few minutes.

Finally giving up, he returned to the car, shifting back to human form on his way. He found her curled on her side across the front seat, fast asleep. Her red tresses seemed to glow in the moonlight and he couldn't resist reaching down to stroke her cheek to discover if her skin was as delicate as it looked.

It was.

He had so many questions that needed to be answered but, for now, he just wanted to taste the curve of her neck below her jaw. He moved in next to her, inhaling her spicy scent, licking her curves as he went.

She stirred and mumbled his name in her sleep but didn't awaken. He liked the roll of his name from her tongue. *Mmm*. Stroking her back in a light massage, he lifted her hair away from her neck to continue his tasty adventure, revealing a small tan birthmark at the base of her head he instantly recognized as the mark of a mate.

Startled, he yanked his fingers away. "What the fuck is that?" When her body jerked awake at his booming voice, he caught sight of the Glock curled in her hand he'd failed to notice before.

Not concerned about the gun or in giving her time to react, he continued, "You have the mark of the cougar on your neck. Who the hell are you?" His heart thumped in his chest, a tell tale sign he was going into a full-blown rage as the implications of her birthmark began to sink in.

Rolling over to face his anger directly, she rested the gun on the seat beside her and spoke plainly. "I am Akira MacDonald of Clan MacDonald of Dragon Tail. I've been trying to tell you for two days who I am, but you either refuse to listen or the time wasn't right to keep pushing."

His eyes narrowed and brow creased into a scowl as he processed her big revelation.

"You should have tried harder."

She shrugged. What had seemed impossible before

was now proven true by the mark she carried, which only complicated the situation. His back stiffened. "If what you said is true and you're part of the Dragon Tail clans, then you've committed the ultimate betrayal of your kind. Your actions are punishable by death in any of the clans and a hunter will be dispatched to pass judgment on you. One of my hunters, in fact." He slammed his fist into the dash, relishing the pain. "Why the hell would you betray us like that? You have to be one cold fucking bitch."

"Whoa, what the hell are you talking about?" she demanded. "I haven't committed any crimes."

"The fact you're working with a group responsible for kidnapping me and who have been trying for days to make me shift on command makes you guilty of the ultimate clan betrayal. I don't even have to give you a trial." He shook his head as he pushed through the car door away from her and paced across the parking lot. "Not to mention I'm a Guardian. Don't you realize how serious this is? No one takes a Death Enforcer and gets away with it. *No one.*"

He needed to get away from her. This was even worse than he'd originally imagined. He or one of his brothers would be responsible for taking her life. Deserving or not, he didn't know how he could handle that. Rage and heat consumed him and every instinctive bone in his body screamed to protect her, take her...claim her.

EIGHTEEN

A s he walked away, Kira opted to let him go —for now.

His posture was rigid, awkward even, as if he was uncomfortable in his own skin. She'd seen the same kind of righteous look in her own clan members when they'd made their decision with no thought to basic right or wrong, consequences be damned. This shit had to stop. They were not Gods.

She stepped from the car, grabbing the keys, but leaving the gun to rest on the seat underneath her purse. Her point would be lost if she accidentally shot the bastard, deserving or not.

"Hey, Lucas." She called out to him, stopping him in his tracks. "I don't think so. You don't get to rage at me and make all kinds of wild accusations and then just walk away. Who the hell do you think *you* are?" She was steaming mad and a freight train couldn't stop her now.

"You invaded my dreams days ago—*my dreams*, got it? All because i've got this fucked up thing in my head that is supposed to be some Goddess given talent. That's bullshit, you know. It's a curse. And damn it—I thought you were just a figment of my imagination. But then the dreams didn't stop, and when I dreamt *you* were in danger I decided to investigate and found *you* in a godforsaken cell. A cell, I might add, I let *you* escape from."

He turned back to face her and she moved right into his personal space, leaving no question how angry she really was. His vivid green and gold eyes were completely unreadable, as he stood there and said nothing. Somehow void of emotion.

"I don't even have a clue as to who did that to you or why you were captured in the first place. I only know of your clan and, by association, I felt obligated to help you. Clan secrets are as important to me as they are to you. Why else would I spend my time in the human military if I wasn't there as the eyes and ears of our councils?" She paused again, waiting for him to say something, and still she got nothing. "To hell with this and to hell with you. I don't need this and I certainly don't need you." Stalking away, she knew that wasn't true, but she had no intention of telling him now. Asshole.

He knew the truth about her and there was no way he'd want her now. She had half a mind to leave him here stranded and half naked on the side of the road in a godforsaken rest area. If he wanted to get home so bad, he could find his own damned way.

CHAPTER
NINETEEN

Lucas paced. He reeled with the implications of her revelation. As Guardian of his clan, it was his duty to know and understand all of the Dragon Tail clans.

Clan MacDonald was a tight knit community of psychics with a wide range of psi abilities. None were shapeshifters. But they were still a powerful race. Dreamwalking was a very common MacDonald trait, so it didn't surprise him she'd be in his dreams and even visioning more with her magical connection to the Tallan.

He stopped short, realization suddenly dawning on him as he remembered the specific session of his study covering the female dreamwalking abilities. In psi clans, sexual dreamwalking only occurred at the onset of mating and only possible with their true mate. It was nature's way for them to find each other.

Oh, shit. No. No. No. There had to be a mistake. It couldn't be true. He struggled for another answer.

Not only was it impossible, it was against their laws.

The uneasy treaty between all the clans clearly stated there would be no interclan breeding.

But deep down, he *knew*. All the unsettled feelings, the burning need, the insatiable hunger. Fate didn't make mistakes, but she sure liked to fuck with people.

I am her mate.

Looking around, he realized he'd walked in a circle and was nearly back at the car. Kira stood propped against the hood— tanned, long, smooth legs on display from hip to ankles, contrasting sharply with the baby blue color of her car. With the certain knowledge of being her mate, he took in her appearance in a whole new light, as if he'd never seen her before.

Suddenly starved, all he wanted for dinner was her. Her arms were crossed in front of her body, a sure sign of her displeasure, but little did she know crossing her arms like that caused her breasts to swell at the edge of her tank top.

She must have been cold, too, as her nipples strained against the thin green fabric. Oh, how he wanted to touch them, roll them between his fingertips and rough them up with a flick of his tongue. His gaze moved up to her face and realized while he'd been fantasizing about her nipples, she'd been glaring at him from beneath those inky lashes. Her eyes narrowed in disapproval.

"I'll take you home, but that's as far as I'll go. I'm done here." Though she spoke in a near whisper, her voice sounded tense and angry, her eyes filled with sadness.

"Kira, you know, don't you? You know I'm your mate." Saying it out loud caused his chest to constrict and he struggled to take in enough air. He hadn't intended on claiming a mate for a very long time, if ever. He liked to play and control way too much.

"I don't care. We don't even like each other. We can't get along for five minutes unless sex is involved. Forget about it. I'm taking you home and then I'm going to forget all about you."

Unbelievable. Arrogant little wench wants to blow this off? "Oh, we are definitely going to the Dragon, but you are going home with *me*. We'll have to come to some sort of agreement regarding our situation. The council will have to be consulted. Even they can't deny the mating mark."

"Pfft. Whatever. Those old bastards can't be trusted. Oh and by the way, here's your agreement." She raised her hand and flipped him the bird. "Fuck off! I don't want you, you don't want me. It's a no-brainer."

God, her mouth really pissed him off and turned him on. She sounded almost irrational now. In fact, in his mind, she was working her way to a punishment. And his brand of punishment she was not likely to forget.

"Get in the car before I do something we'll both regret. We're leaving."

CHAPTER
TWENTY

Hours later, Kira found herself drifting towards sleep she didn't want. She'd reluctantly allowed Lucas to drive her car as they headed back to the Dragon.

They hadn't spoken since they'd gotten back on the highway, and the miles of blacktop passing in front of them lulled her toward sleep. The place she feared the most right now. One of two things would happen, and neither appealed to her at the moment.

Dreamwalking with Lucas, although unlikely since he was wide-awake behind the wheel, or some alternate version of reality that accompanied her degenerative mating period.

The curse of the female psychic. The stronger her power grew, the worse it seemed to affect her at this point. She doubted he knew, since it was the one secret or weakness her clan did not want revealed.

Thank God. That's all she needed. Him mating with her

out of pity or worse. Her shoulders shook at the mere thought.

So she fought sleep, despite the exhaustion setting in. Maybe a little catnap would work. She laughed at her own pun, glancing furtively to the side to see if Lucas watched her. His profile looked set in stone. He stared out the front windshield, unmoving, his mouth set in a grim line. She wanted inside his head but he'd firmly locked her out. Whatever he was thinking would remain private for now. She let her eyes slide shut. Even he had to sleep sometime...

What does Lucas want from me? He's forcing me to his home. For what? He must think if we mate he'll be able to control me. Will he take advantage of me again? I need to come up with a plan before we get there.

If his clan catches me there, they will claim me and I'll never be allowed to return home. God forbid if he has any brothers or close pride mates, I'll become a sex slave to them all.

Good thing I'm a trained soldier. They may be stronger thanks to their supernatural cat powers, but they still have no idea who they're dealing with.

No man is going to claim me and have me slave to his every need. My mother put up with that for so many years. That will never be me. Didn't she realize I was there when he took her over and over again until she nearly died from it? Why didn't she try to take us away?

A deep feline snarl sounded from somewhere behind her. *I have to run, I have to hide. Now...*

• • •

THE CAR STOPPED and Kira snapped awake. Her thoughts were cloudy and she couldn't seem to focus. Only one thought lingered. *Must get away, find a place to hide. Don't go with him anymore.*

Need to run.

Lucas opened her door and she stepped out of the car onto the soft, muddy ground. The dirt was red, reminding her of the red clay of North Carolina. *Home.*

Looking up, she noticed they'd parked in front of a small cabin nestled in the trees at the base of a mountain. The color and texture of the structure blended with the terrain, creating a natural camouflage, probably preventing anyone from spotting it at a distance. A good spot to hide.

"Where are we?" Just then she noticed a tall, handsome man approaching them, and she nervously looked at Lucas. Sweat broke out on her forehead as she took a couple of steps backwards, sinking into the mud.

"This is my home."

The other man moved closer, a grin splitting across his handsome face. That kind of good looks probably got him whatever he wanted and left a string of broken hearts behind. When he came within reach, Lucas pulled the man to him for a friendly hug.

"Lucas, it's about damn time you got back here." The stranger turned to her and drank her in like a fine wine. Slow and careful. "And who is this you've brought with you? A present for me?"

"Hardly, asshole. Kane, this is Akira. Akira, this is Kane, my youngest brother.

"Half brother actually, which explains why I am so much better looking than Lucas here." Kane's response and smile were lost on her as an illogical fear gripped her, squeezing in on her like an inescapable vise.

CHAPTER
TWENTY-ONE

At the word *brother*, Kira's heart rate had sped up and her face clouded in obvious distress. She jerked her hand away from him, turned and without uttering a single word, ran into the woods.

"Kira, what are you doing? What's wrong?" She didn't answer and he looked at Kane with an incredulous face and just shrugged.

Kane laughed. "Having trouble keeping your women nowadays, big brother? You must be turning into a really scary guy if they're desperate enough to take off running through the woods."

"Shut up and take this inside. I'll be back in a minute." He tossed Kira's duffle bag to his brother and took off in the direction she had run. As he left the drive, he heard Kane's mocking laugh behind him.

Has was so going to paddle her ass for this.

Kira. He spoke, pushing into her mind. Her panic and fear pushed back at him. *What the hell is going on? Why are you running away?*

I—I can't let you claim me. I won't be like her. Ever.

Her? What? Her response may have confused him, but it was her panic that crawled along his skin, scaring the hell out of him. *Babe, what are you talking about? Her? What her?*

She didn't answer and he sensed nothing. In fact, it was as if she'd disappeared or, worse, didn't exist. He reached for her with everything he had and got nothing. Fear clutched his heart and his beast roared forward, demanding control.

He dropped down on all fours and in a blink of any eye, he'd shifted. He'd catch up with her quicker this way, not to mention his senses were sharper for tracking. He sprang onto the overhanging cliff and began his search.

Lucas suspected something was terribly wrong. A shiver worked along his spine. So far he couldn't identify the danger but he trusted his instincts to know when something wasn't right.

Continuing to push his mind, he searched for her, trying to make a connection. He'd lost her scent a while back, which made no sense at all. She'd only had a minute or so head start, how could she have just vanished, scent and all?

The forest was deathly still, giving him the universal sign of something terrible gone wrong. He crossed through the shallow stream, looking for signs of disturbed vegetation along the bank or broken debris, anything that would give him a trail.

At the deepest part of the stream, the frigid water lapped at his furred belly as he picked up speed, determined to find her. When his paws cleared the water and landed on the rocky embankment, he found her, or at least her trail. After several minutes, he reached out for help.

Kane, something is seriously wrong out here.

What? What do you mean?

I'm not sure, but I sense Akira is in grave danger. Every-thing is too quiet. I have her scent and I'm headed for the river right now.

I'm on my way, brother.

Lucas continued to follow her trail. He had picked up an additional familiar female stench that struck true fear in his heart.

That bitch from the lab had followed them somehow and she'd managed to get a hold of his mate.

Whoa, where had that come from? That damned word kept popping into his head. He had to quit thinking of her as a mate. She wasn't his. Yet, considering everything that had happened over the last two days, he realized he wanted more from her. How much, he wasn't sure, but he wasn't ready to let her go...

If that bitch Lara hurts Kira, I will kill her. Then the real hunt would begin because he already knew someone else was pulling her strings, and he had a pretty good idea who was responsible. His enemies underestimated his patience. In time, they would all get what they deserved.

She's in my woods now, and it's payback time.

He snarled at the anticipated pleasure before he put his muzzle to the ground and picked up speed. They were close. *Akira, hold on, baby. I'm coming.*

CHAPTER
TWENTY-TWO

Kira slowly opened her eyes. Her stomach rolled. She lay still, trying to clear her fuzzy thoughts and settle the nausea enough to move. Where was she? She pulled at the edges of her memory for an explanation.

One minute she was in Lucas' car, the next running from Lucas in sheer terror. Her only thought to get as far away as possible. Against a cougar on home turf, she didn't have much of a chance. He'd follow and find her. Her only chance at survival had been to get to the river where she could mask her scent.

Something had stopped her. A tree...no, not a tree. She'd run into a person, a woman. Kira focused harder on the memory and grabbed aimlessly at her neck. She remembered the stinging pain of a needle being plunged into her neck. She'd been drugged by the...her vision cleared...*the bitch from the base*.

Time to get the hell out of dodge. When she attempted to move her arms and legs she couldn't go more than a few inches. She lifted her head and found herself sprawled out on a flat rock with her wrists and ankles bound.

Before she could think any further about her situation, a sudden heave in her stomach forced her to roll her head over to the side and throw up. Her gut cramped as the pain from the drug she'd been hit with rolled through her system.

"What's the matter, honey? You got a weak stomach?" The female voice was so heavy with sarcasm Kira wanted to turn and smack her. She craned her neck farther to the side and caught a glimpse of camouflage clad legs walking around her. Kira couldn't speak with her mouth so dry and parched. The woman knelt down to her level to look her in the eye. "Not to worry your pretty little head, this will all be over soon. When Lucas finds us, I'll recapture what belongs to me and you'll no longer be needed. Although, I bet you would be a lot of fun for *him* to play with."

She had no idea who the crazy bitch referred to but she'd bet her last dime or moment of sanity she wouldn't like *him*.

Contemplating the implications of the woman's words, Kira quickly began calculating her options. After all, this was what she was trained for. She averted her eyes and glanced around the small clearing searching for reinforcements. She saw none. Lying on a rock across the clearing from her was some sort of metal ring and what looked like an electric baton. Probably a stunner of some sort. *Who is this woman who thinks all she needs are a few weak weapons to capture a man like Lucas? What a fool.*

She struggled to sit. Not an easy feat when trussed up like a Thanksgiving turkey. Focused now, she easily functioned through the pain, but she knew the smart move would be to fake incapacity. That would lull her captor into a false sense of complete control, and buy her more time to plan and eventually get away. Rash actions were not Kira's way. For optimal success, if given the opportunity, she always devised a plan.

"What do you want with Lucas?" she meekly asked the guard.

"Ah, would you really like to know?" She smiled at Kira with a sick twist to her face and a strange gleam in her eyes. "How much do you care for him? Enough to save his life?"

Kira considered her question. She did care for him. To what extent, she wasn't sure. He was her mate and, like him or not, love him or not, she didn't want to see him captured again.

"Care for him? Are you crazy? I barely know him."

The woman's dark head snapped up and she studied Kira's eyes, as though searching for something. "I hear lies. He broke Clan rules for you, didn't he? He shifted to save your life. Obviously he wants to protect you. So trying to hide your feelings at this point isn't very clever. I guess I expected too much from you." The woman's face turned to disgust. "No challenge here whatsoever."

Rage swelled inside Kira, twisting deep in her gut. "Touch him and I *will* kill you."

"Ahh, now that's more like it. Still worthless, but more what I expected." The woman snarled as she stomped to the other side of the clearing. Kira didn't like the look of pure hatred in the other woman's eyes. She needed to tread carefully or risk provoking more crazy from this woman.

Unfortunately, her hands were still bound and she had yet to come up with a plan for freeing herself.

What was taking Lucas so long? Had he come after her? What must have went through his head when she took off running at the word *brother*? Kira hung her head. The psychic breaks were getting longer and more frequent, making it difficult to convince herself she was exaggerating or even just plain making up scenarios in her head to frighten herself. With every new episode they got more realistic. She pondered how much longer she had before her mind succumbed to the darkness. Weeks? Days?

Kira...Kira, can you hear me? The faint sound of Lucas' voice drifted through her mind. Faint or not, she heard him, which meant he was looking for her. The drug she'd been injected with had probably been the cause of their link being broken and now that it was wearing off, he was able to get through.

Lucas, stop! Go back! It's a trap!

I know. Kane and I are approaching, but I think she is more than she appears, and it may take us more time than I'd like to get to you. You need to distract her.

I don't know what her actual plan is, but it appears she's waiting, probably expecting you to get here soon. As she responded to Lucas she turned her head and met Lara's wary stare. She looked intense, suspicious, as if she knew something was going on. It sent chills up Kira's spine and she looked quickly away. She was getting that odd feeling again, like outside the motel. Sensing something not right. As if she was missing something important right in front of her. She reached out, searching for a connection to the problem but was unable to pinpoint it.

She heard a woman chuckling and turned quickly to look back at her. She met the woman's gaze, rage against hatred sizzling between them. Still she heard the chuckling.

Kira struggled again to sit up, considering she was still bound and partially naked. "Excuse me, but I need to go to the bathroom." There had to be something she could do to distract her.

Kira watched the woman turn away from the weapons and simply stare at her. She wasn't looking at Kira's face so much as looking through her. Her eyes were glazed over and her dark pupils almost obliterating the rest of the color.

She looked down. With her partially bared breasts peeking through her torn shirt and the eery leer from her captor, Kira got a weird sense she was about to become some sort of twisted sacrifice.

Uh oh, Lucas, you better hurry up. I don't like the look she's giving me and my half naked body. She's creeping me the hell out.

You're naked?

She'd have laughed at his shocked tone if a loon wasn't stalking her. *Sort of.* They didn't have time to worry about the details of her clothing.

I'm coming baby, I'm coming.

Kira watched her captor move as fear threatened to engulf her. The woman picked up one of her weapons and walked over to Kira.

"Don't think you can play games with me." She grasped Kira by the hair, pulling her close, and clamped some sort of heavy-duty vise with what looked like claws attached to the rim around her left nipple.

Before her brain could register the effect she repeated with another on the right. Kira screamed loudly, tears springing to her eyes at the excruciating pain.

Leaning down, the woman wrapped one hand around her neck, choking off her air supply. Kira couldn't speak. She couldn't think. She didn't have much time.

"Don't worry, sweetheart. How much pain you endure is completely up to you. You tell me what I want to know and it stops. You don't tell me and well..." the woman shrugged letting Kira draw her own conclusions as the fire streaking across her breasts made her vision blur.

"Now tell me. Where is he? I know he's close. Tell him to back off, or you die here and now," she snarled viciously at Kira. "His surrender will come on my terms, not his."

Kira tried to struggle but the pain was too intense. Black spots wavered in front of her eyes. The woman slammed Kira's head against the rock, adding to the already mind numbing pain. This couldn't be the end. She refused to go out this way.

"While you helped my cause immensely, I didn't plan to kill you." She bent closer. "Vengeance is mine."

Fuck you, Kira mouthed.

Without warning, two big cats leapt from the trees above. The larger, midnight black one leaped on the woman's back and its jaws clamped down on her neck. The woman's eyes bulged in shock and silently pleaded with her.

Kira felt the weight of both the woman and the cat pressing down on her and heard the woman's neck bones crushing next to her ear. Without releasing its grip of the woman's neck, the cougar pulled her off of Kira and threw her across the clearing in the direction of the other cat.

Kira gulped for breath as the cougar shifted back to his human form and she found herself lost in the blazing green and gold eyes of her mate. "Quick," she croaked out, "get these off me." She tried to wave in the direction of her chest.

"Keep breathing, Akira. This is going to hurt more." Lucas deftly grabbed the devices and released her. She cried out. The sudden flow of blood rushing to the tips burned as much if not worse than the original pain of the device. Tears streamed down her face as she endured.

"It's okay, baby." He massaged the sides of her breasts with a soft, experienced touch. "It's normal to be more intense when they're first released. It will only last a few minutes. I promise."

"Do I even want to know how you know that?"

"We'll have plenty of time for me to explain." He untied her hands and feet and threw the ropes into the woods. Their gazes locked on each other, neither able to speak and Kira knew she couldn't possibly tell Lucas what she felt. Not now. Confusion swirled inside her. She needed him as much as she didn't want to need him. If she were smart, she'd run as far and as fast as she could. This wouldn't work...

Kira sprang into his arms, seeking the comfort and heat she so desperately needed. She threw her arms around his neck and wrapped her legs around his torso. From the waist up, the contact between them was mostly skin-to-skin, heat to heat, and the rest of his male naked flesh pressed against the thin silk barrier of her panties.

She banished the memory of her shorts being sliced from her body and the ripped and torn tank she still wore on her shoulders. Instead she forced her mind to focus on the more pleasurable wave of need and lust coming from Lucas and the haunted look in his eyes. They needed each other, needed to cling to the powerful emotions of burning heat driven by fate.

"I'm so sorry it took me so long to get here," he said.

She shook her head, still unable to form words as the scalding flood of emotions from the past two days engulfed her.

Adrenalin coursed through every vein, pushing everything else away, leaving her raw and open. Hot flames of desire licked at her skin when Lucas wrapped his hand around the back of her neck and slanted his mouth over hers, licking and nibbling at her lips.

The taste and heat of his kiss flooded her and brief thoughts of her mating call flared up again. She wanted him, her body so hot she feared she might combust, but the thought of him becoming her mate without love scared her to death.

She liked him. Despite the stubbornness he displayed at every turn, she sensed his intentions were honest and true. Yes, she was attracted to him, craved him even, but she didn't love him any more than he loved her.

When his tongue slid between her lips, she moaned at the delicious friction he created with the rough texture of his tongue.

How was she supposed to deny this?

Her arms tightened around his neck as he devoured her mouth and pulled her tight against him, his rigid erection fitting perfectly between the juncture of her thighs. She liked the possessive way he held her, rubbed against her, as if seeking more touch and more pleasure for them both.

"If we don't stop now, I will take you right here," he warned, his voice rough and dark, sending a direct pulse of pleasure straight to her center. His free hand cupped her breast, tracing the skin to her sore nipple where he gently caressed the tender area, wiping away the lingering pain.

"I don't care."

He trailed kisses from her jaw to her neck and onward until his warm breath floated across the puckered flesh of her taut nipple. He moved against her hips, his shaft rubbing the full length of her damp heat.

Wetness pooled against her panties and, so help her, she wanted him right here and right now. No waiting. No thinking about what they should be doing. Or if this was the right thing. Now. Only him. Nothing mattered beyond the need of having him inside her right now.

"I'm not sure I can be gentle this time." His breathing sounded labored as she imagined him fighting for control. "The animal in me wants to mount you, take you hard. You're mine, damn it."

"It's okay. I'm okay"

"No, it's not. I should have protected you."

"You saved me." She bit at his flat, pointed nipples then. Hard nips that made him unleash a series of growls. A sexy, possessive sound rumbled through his chest. Her sex clenched, more moisture spilling onto her sensitive skin.

His nostrils flared and she knew he smelled the extent of her arousal. She unwrapped her arms and legs from around him, nearly tumbling them to the ground. She hastily jerked her panties from her legs and relaxed back against the rock, lifting herself up to part her thighs just enough.

"Kiss me, Lucas, I need you." The sound he made should have worried her, but it didn't. This primal, nature of his animal half touched something deep and dark inside her. A place that created liquid fire in her body at every thought of her mate. Something that refused to be denied.

His hand snaked out and reached between her thighs, running his fingers through her kinky curls. His fingers swirled through the moisture and slipped inside.

"Yes!" she hissed through clenched teeth, drowning in the pleasure of friction surging over her. That simple jolt nearly threw her over the edge. Her climax was already building, and if he hit just the right spot...

His head bent to her apex and he lapped at her. The breath left Kira's lungs, leaving her unable to utter a sound. His lips wrapped around her clit and sucked while he used his fingers to make her wild. She heard herself scream as the passion flooded through her and she hit the point of no return, tumbling head first over the edge.

She pulsed around his fingers and writhed against his mouth, light and flame overtaking her senses. So wrapped up in the haze of her orgasm, she was surprised to find herself flipped onto her belly, Lucas pressing against her backside before sliding lower to nudge her opening. Rough hands dug into her hips as he worked his length inside in short, hard thrusts.

"Yes, please—please," she begged for more.

He sank balls deep inside her slick channel, pushing her against the rock and sending jolts of pleasure racing through her. She faced forward, searching for something to grab onto for leverage and came face to face with Kane who stood about twenty feet off to the side, watching. In her desperation and need for Lucas she'd forgotten she had seen two big cats.

His dark beauty entranced and fascinated her as she studied the light in his eyes as he watched. She had never had someone watch her do something so intimate. It both unnerved her and made her stomach tremble with excitement.

With every pulse and thrust of Lucas inside her, teasing her nerve endings and sensitive walls, she came closer and closer to the edge again. Faster and faster Lucas took her, until he swelled inside her. Her eyes slid shut as she held on to that rock for dear life. All while she writhed beneath him, pushing against his hips, forcing him as deep as possible.

The heat built impossibly high until her orgasm exploded and she screamed out his name. His release hit at the same time as he jerked against her. As Lucas pulsed inside her she opened her eyes to find the small clearing empty with Kane nowhere in sight. He'd disappeared as quietly as he'd appeared and she refused to examine how that made her feel. Her life was too short to start obsessing over regret now.

As the waves of aftershocks began to fade, Kira collapsed onto the rock. Too satisfied and too tired to feel bad about what had happened or the fact she had momentarily enjoyed the fact someone had watched, she closed her eyes and thought of her mate. When they had come together, her body had once again burned for him to complete the mating ritual. Instinct had demanded it.

She had even experienced a moment of anger when he didn't bite her.

Now that the fever had begun to cool, she didn't know what to think or how to process these feelings. Instead, she kept her eyes closed, afraid to look at Lucas and see regret while she still felt the dark pleasure of him coursing through her veins.

Lucas slid from her body and gathered her in his arms. "Akira, come home with me. Let me take you to my bed, feel you safe in my arms. I need more time," Lucas whispered in her ear.

His voice sounded ragged and confused, just like she felt. She nodded against his chest, not ready to speak. Afraid to break the tenuous bond they had just formed. At her consent, he picked her up and began carrying her home.

TWENTY-THREE

L ucas worried. So much so that he'd walked away from Kane, leaving him to deal with the mess. But killing Lara while on top of Kira had scared the shit out of him. She had looked so pale and frightened. Yet he'd taken her as if he had never been with another woman. Adrenaline and emotion had been high and the urge to mate with her had been a compelling force. Just as he'd been about to come he'd looked down at her neck, the mark calling out to him.

His mouth had watered with the need to bite into her succulent flesh in the one spot that would change their lives forever. Thank God for Kane and his presence. Catching a glimpse of him across the clearing in that crucial moment had provided enough of a distraction to keep him from doing something both he and Kira would later regret.

She made him feel and he wasn't too sure if that was a good thing or not. He had to maintain control at all times and unnecessary attachments were out of the question. He had a tough job and sometimes it got ugly. That didn't make him a lot of friends.

He turned to look at her sleeping form. Would he want to take her as a mate? It didn't matter. His clan would never allow it. Shapeshifters did not mix well and were forbidden to mate with other races. It was one of the many reasons they isolated themselves from other clans.

Kira stirred, mumbling something in her sleep he couldn't quite understand. He ran his fingers through her hair and spoke softly to her trying to comfort her as he would a child, but touching her like this caused his blood to heat. He definitely couldn't get enough of her. She'd tormented his dreams for so long and now here she was: all soft flesh and beautiful heat. He lowered his head down to hers and touched her lips with his own for a gentle kiss. They were silky soft and slightly swollen from their earlier encounter.

He needed to know what they would feel like wrapped around his cock? That image caused a slight growl to escape his lips.

Would you like me to show you?

He started, not expecting her to have heard his thoughts. She giggled and her eyes popped open. "It's hard to get any rest around here when all you can think about is sex."

He rolled on top of her, pinning her in place. "You little minx. Don't you know it's not polite to listen to others' private thoughts?" he growled. He pressed against her leg as she squirmed around, trying to get out from under him.

"Is that a no?" she asked. Before he could answer she got a leg out and around him, flipping him onto his back.

She straddled his hips, raking his naked torso inch by inch with her inquisitive gaze. From a distance he knew his chest appeared hairless, but in reality there was a layer of blond fur that covered every inch of him.

"It's so soft. I've never felt anything like it." Bending to take one of his hardened nipples between her teeth, she smoothed her hands over his muscled abs. Her hot mouth exploring his skin drove him insane. He needed to be inside her, filling her. Wanted to feel him stretching her again. Desperate to touch her again, he traced his fingers along the sensitive skin of her side, admiring the dip of her waist and outward curve of her hips. He rested his hands on her waist, reaching his fingers around her body. Their bodies fit, like they were made for each other. Amazing.

She bit at his nipples again, back and forth between the two, sending shivers of sexual need straight to his aching cock. When her lips began a trail down to his belly, his hands bit into her waist as he fought the urge to take her with violence.

She wanted this time to explore and he would try to give it to her, even if it killed him.

She reached for his buckle and unfastened his pants. "I don't understand why you even bothered to dress." His cock sprang free, bouncing against his abs before she fisted him with both hands. He sucked in a sharp breath, silently pleading with her to let him fuck her mouth. Yeah, this kind of restraint was not in his nature.

She bent down and cautiously licked around the tip, the skin pulled tight and throbbing for release. A drop of cum beaded at the top and she greedily licked him clean.

He tried thrusting his hips to get inside her mouth, but she held fast and refused to be rushed.

"Be patient. You'll get your turn to be in control later." She eyed him wickedly as he arched his eyebrow.

"I don't give up control to anyone, Kira. It's not who I am."

"Then don't think about it as control. Instead you'll be letting me please you in my own way."

He paused, considering her request before assenting. "Only if you let me play, too." He saw the moment she realized what he was talking about. A sly smile curved her lips upwards.

"Deal."

Wiggling her body around so she could get to him from a different angle, she thrust her ass in the air, positioning her glistening pussy right in front of his face.

Fuck yeah. He stroked her hips, savoring the moment before he dove in.

On a moan she engulfed him all the way to the back of her throat. "Ooh, fuck! Yes." He grabbed her ass to keep himself from shooting off the bed as she began sucking him in and out of her mouth.

He needed a distraction to regain some control or this would all be over in a matter of minutes. He stroked two fingers along her slick folds before pushing them into her opening. Her satiny walls caressed him as he curved upward searching for her inner sweet spot, the one that would make her quiver and beg and forget all about being in charge.

When her lower body jerked against his face, he knew he'd found it. He flicked it a few times to watch her reaction and then started a stroke in and out of her in a strong but slow movement, designed to tease and torment her sweet heat.

He smiled when her muscles squeezed around his fingers as he picked up the pace and fucked her harder.

She responded by grazing her teeth along his shaft, causing his muscles to clench in fevered agony. He tilted his head up and ran his tongue along her entire slit, up one side and down the other, paying close attention to her gorgeous clit with every pass.

She moaned around him.

Sucking him in as deep as she could take it, Kira kept a tight fist at the base. She felt his orgasm rising as his shaft swelled even more with each pulse. Encouraged by his reactions, she thrust her lips around him faster. His fingers and tongue were driving her wild and she couldn't hold back much longer. The direct pressure he continued to apply on her G-spot with every stroke was more than she could bear.

She was losing control... Her orgasm burst free around his fingers and her muscles convulsed, clutching him tightly.

At nearly the same time he pulsed in her mouth and flooded her with his release. She continued to suck and lick as fast as she could until she'd taken every last drop and he slumped against the mattress.

His fingers slipped from her as her knees buckled and she fell limp across his strong thighs.

For a few blissful moments she basked in the feelings

of euphoria they created together. There was no denying he completed her and the urge to tell him, share the moment overwhelmed her. Her mouth opened and then snapped shut. What the hell was she thinking? How could she forget her problems? Like slamming into a brick wall— her body locked up.

"Kira, what's wrong?" He sounded so worried.

She rolled off of him and grasped the sheet, covering her breasts. "Nothing." She couldn't tell him. Wouldn't take away his choice. In the long run he'd resent it and she would eventually pay for that. "I just want to get cleaned up." Tears welled in her eyes that she desperately wanted to hide. Yanking the sheet around her body, she practically ran to the bathroom, slamming the door behind her.

CHAPTER
TWENTY-FOUR

Malcolm paced around his office. It had been twenty-four hours since he'd heard from Lara and it was unsettling to say the least. The idiot little witch probably screwed up again and didn't want to tell him.

Looking down at his hands, he realized he'd been clenching his fists so tight he had broken the skin.

God, not having his powers drove him crazy. He wanted to reach for her telepathically and couldn't. He wanted to run wild and free through the woods in his cougar form, and couldn't. It was pure misery being forced to live like a mortal, but with a raging beast inside him always fighting to get free.

It was way past time to find a solution. The debilitating pain of a caged animal diminished his strength and the only control he still maintained was his hold over the witch who worked with him. Fortunately, no one else had noticed the change in his abilities either and still feared the wrath of a former Death Enforcer. However, that tenuous hold wouldn't last forever.

His brothers alone held the answers he sought, but were not willing to go against the council to even speak to him. Their lack of faith and inability to stand on their own would eventually lead to their downfall.

He'd kept his part in Lucas' capture a secret in the hope that lack of information would eventually lead to him lowering his guard. It did not.

Now he would have to rethink his strategy once he had his hands on his brother again. Dealing with his family's ignorance for all of these years had to come to an end.

Sure, he had dabbled in the dark arts with a few witches in his time, but he hadn't planned on risking exposure to mortals by doing so. But in his eyes the punishment most certainly did not fit the crime.

Those witches had been such fun. They were the most sexually adventurous women he'd met.

Unlike the uptight feline bitches of his clan. Remembering his last attempt at a little light bondage with a feline made the scars on his back itch. He had needed more. He'd ached to be in complete control of every aspect of his life, and for a while those three witches had fulfilled all of his desires. He should have known they couldn't be trusted to keep his secrets.

Just like Lara. Another dark witch who had promised to help him. Like him, she'd been banished by her Coven and even the other dark witches feared her. In the past she'd been eager to serve him, but recently—in fact, ever since he had gotten her to capture Lucas—he sensed her evasiveness. She seemed to have an agenda he couldn't uncover and now seemingly had gone off the plan and on her own.

"Dammit, I have to find her and it looks like I'll have to do it myself." But, first things first. He had to do something about the crippling pain locked inside him.

So far he'd found only one way to a temporary reprieve and just thinking about how to punish Lara when he found her had his dick rock hard and desperate for release.

He needed a clear head and a plan to go after his family and his wayward witch and for that he needed a partner.

Thinking over the possibilities, he called for Krissy to join him in his office. He opened the bottom drawer of his desk and withdrew the restraints and his thick leather whip.

Krissy would have to endure Lara's punishment for now.

The door slid quietly open and the voluptuous Krissy sauntered in. She was dressed in combat gear, having just come from the training field. Her tank top molded to her large breasts, showing her peaked nipples. Her snug camouflage pants barely concealed what he knew to be long, lean legs. He imagined spreading those legs wide and tying them down to his bed one at a time.

They'd look even better with red welts striping them. His cock stiffened more. When she was tied up and help-less, her body would ache in anticipation. Hot tears would streak her face as she begged for him to whip her more.

Maybe this time he'd tie her down on her stomach instead and drive into her hot, tight ass. Yes, that would be just the way to gain her submission.

Of course, not until she begged. The animal's rage inside him would settle for no less.

"Strip now," Malcolm demanded.

"But, Mal—" He cut her off with a jerk of her arm.

"I am your master and you will not speak to me unless spoken to, do you understand?" He waited for her answer while he watched her emotions flicker through her eyes.

Sure, he made her angry when he demanded total obedience, but he also recognized desire. She had been worked long and hard to get in his bed for quite some time, but mistakenly thought she would do it on her own terms.

The memory made him want to chuckle, but he held it in. There was no humor to be found in this dark and desperate act. The depravity that held the pain at bay came at a very high price and he understood that the day would come to pay.

But today was not that day.

He returned his focus to the woman standing in front of him with her eyes cast to the floor. She had come to understand he would only accept her if she was willing to surrender one hundred percent.

"Strip," he repeated.

"Yes, sir," she whispered, putting down her weapons as she began removing her clothes.

Oh yes, today her submission and payment for Lara's latest betrayal was going to be very, very sweet.

TWENTY-FIVE

L ucas padded quietly along the forest floor, searching. His paws were sensitive to every blade of grass, fallen leaf, or patch of mud, making him capable of discerning even the smallest change in the environment. He had been following an unusual scent for over an hour now and had to be getting close to finding the source.

When Kane told him Lara's body had gone missing, he had left Kira with him and set out to search. He'd returned to the scene of the crime and retraced her death. How could a dead body disappear within minutes of the fight and with two powerful hunters nearby? However it happened, he knew for certain he had to find her before some stray hunter did and put out a call for help. The last thing they needed were the locals poking around their woods and asking questions.

He'd left his brother behind to take care of the woman not only because he needed someone to watch out for Kira, but also to give his brother some time to sort out what he'd seen. For the first time in he didn't know how long, he had lost control with a woman.

He wanted to explain, but how did you do that when you didn't even understand the change yourself? Everything about Kira seemed different from any woman he'd been with before and he didn't want to believe it all had to do with the mark on the back of her neck. Right now emotions were running high and more than ever he needed to focus on his job.

Lucas let the early, cool mountain air ripple over his fur, regulating his body temperature as he continued his pursuit of the offensive scent. It didn't smell like the witch but it carried an evil stench in a similar manner that made his stomach turn in disgust. *Who was he following? And what had they decided to do about Lara?*

The memory of Lara's hands wrapped around Kira's neck, choking her, burned in his blood again. Killing her so quickly hadn't been enough. She should have suffered like she'd made Kira suffer. As she had made him suffer.

His need to protect Kira had grown exponentially in the last twenty-four hours and, despite taking her several times, he was nowhere near satisfied. He wanted more, needed to have her again and again. He wanted to plunge into her wetness, savor her unique sweet flavor, watch her lips wrap around him again... And he loved the way her eyes glowed with pleasure when she came.

What would it take to satisfy his hunger with her? Would it ever be enough?

He had to be careful. If the Council found out a rival clan member was staying with him and that he was her potential mate, there'd be serious consequences for him.

Who was he kidding? They would find out. It was just a matter of time. You couldn't hide secrets in the Tail of the Dragon; they whispered on the wind. And when they found out, they would never accept an official mating between the clans.

Demands would be made. Lines drawn.

To his surprise, Kira had not spoken to him about the mating ritual or their fate. Didn't she care enough about him to consider the possibility?

Unless she already came to the same realization he had and decided it wasn't meant to be. His chest constricted at the thought of Kira leaving him to return to her home.

He had to stop moving to take some deep breaths and shake the heavy, ominous sensation. He struggled with thoughts of unexpected pain and discomfort as he absorbed the implications of her leaving as well as her staying.

Why did that make him uncomfortable? Not once had he ever needed or wanted a permanent companion. He enjoyed his solitude too much and could never be happy without it. Right?

TWENTY-SIX

Kira looked around the room, contemplating what to do first. Restless since she'd heard Lucas leave, she searched for ideas.

Admiring his cabin, she walked into the kitchen. A small pine table sat in the corner with only one chair underneath it.

Everything was put away and the place was as neat as a pin, which totally freaked her out. How could someone be this neat? Even the military didn't expect this from her.

The cabinets looked hand carved and the soft, earthy colors soothed her frazzled nerves and encouraged her to relax and take some time to explore. It was obvious only one person lived here by the lack of duplicates.

His dishes didn't come in sets, only a solitary towel hung in the bathroom and the living room only contained the bare essentials of furniture. She guessed Lucas didn't entertain much and instead spent a great deal of time alone.

She understood that. When you don't feel like you fit

in, you choose to separate yourself from others rather than share a lot of awkward moments. Yeah, not like she knew anything about that.

Her relationships with men to date had never lasted more than one night. Of that she made sure. She loved having sex, lots of sex, and looked forward to every encounter. As long as it ended in the morning.

Now, being drawn to her mate time and time again made it almost impossible to walk away. She found that she burned for him every waking moment. She wanted him buried deep inside her at every opportunity. Just thinking of him now caused her sex to spasm, making her slick and ready. What would happen when one or both of them walked away?

Well, she knew what would happen to her physically, but what about her heart? Was she falling in love with him this quick? Could she ever trust him?

Not if he kept leaving her in the dark like this, expecting her to wait for him. She needed to be out, helping him find that bitch's dead body, but he'd snuck out without her.

What a waste of time for him and Kane to try to hide their conversation from her by whispering outside. She had no problem walking through minds when she had a mission to accomplish or if she just plain needed to find out what was going on.

She'd heard all the shocking details about the missing body and Kane's fruitless search. If Lucas had trusted her with this information, he would have seen she was perfectly capable of helping him accomplish any job. Just because she couldn't shift didn't mean her abilities weren't useful.

She'd had a close call with Lara, which left her with the need for some payback. Sure, Lucas eliminated Lara quickly, but in hindsight it would have been a better idea to attempt an interrogation to find out who else was involved before taking such drastic measures. Kira thought about the excruciating pain she'd endured and imagined how much worse it might have gotten if Lucas hadn't arrived when he had.

Chills raced across her body, raising gooseflesh on her arms. She had a bad feeling this was far from over. She needed to return to the latest crime scene and appropriate some intel, conduct a proper investigation. Ignoring her instincts would be a mistake.

Now that she had a plan, she reached out for Kane's location so she could slip past him. Lucas had asked him to stay and keep an eye on her. She shook her head and chuckled. "Men." They just had no idea. Realizing he was sitting in the rocker on the front porch, she slipped out the side door in the kitchen without a sound. He and Lucas were probably going to be pissed when they discovered her gone, but hey, that was their problem.

CHAPTER
TWENTY-SEVEN

L ucas continued to trail the scent for hours and still nothing. No body, no other people, nothing but a strange smell.

He had looped back around and was now only a few kilometers from his home and Kira. He longed to be with her again. To touch her, make her squirm and scream in ecstasy. His pace quickened in anticipation. Would she be spread out on his bed, waiting? Or would she be curled up with a pillow, giving him a delectable view of her full, heart shaped ass that he had an unholy love of?

His thoughts had frequently strayed to that luscious ass and he wondered if she would let him take her there. He imagined easing into her tight rosebud, seating himself to his balls. He just knew her ass would grip him so tight he'd have to use every ounce of control not to come instantly.

Through the trees he caught sight of his cabin. He jumped onto the ground and sprinted toward the house, anxious to be with his woman. He might have to consider sending out a tracker to search for the missing witch, considering neither he nor Kane had located her.

The council would also have to be notified of his return and briefed on the circumstances of his capture and escape. Once he reported in, hiding Kira would no longer be an option, but having a missing body somewhere in his woods would only endanger them all. His role required action no matter the consequences.

He shifted back to human form as his paws hit the front steps.

Kane sat outside, waiting for him to return. When he caught sight of Lucas he stood to greet him and stopped short. When he started howling with laughter, Lucas remembered he was naked from the shift and fully aroused.

A glance down confirmed his predicament. He shrugged That's what his mate did to him. He raised his head and locked gazes with his brother. Fuck it. It wasn't as if Kane hadn't seem him like this before.

"Hey, bro, you having a little problem?" Kane snickered while nodding his head down to Lucas' groin.

"Yeah, one I'm about to rectify. So thanks for your help, but hit the road."

"Uhm...yeah...about that..."

CHAPTER
TWENTY-EIGHT

Kira traveled through the dense forest for hours, trying to locate the original scene, methodically searching the brush and scattered debris along the way as well as her mind for much needed clues. Finally stepping into the clearing, she let the surge of sudden anger that had remained on the scene wash over her.

Humiliation burned her face as she remembered how easily Lara had gotten the best of her despite her extensive training. Her psychic powers were declining too rapidly. It even affected her physical abilities. Time was definitely running out for her.

After a few more minutes of self-indulgent venting, Kira moved over to the rock across the clearing from where she'd been sitting. She remembered seeing some sort of objects resting on the rocks she thought had been weapons.

Lara had turned her back on her and spent a good deal of time fiddling with the items that had rested on the rock. Where had they gone when Lara had been killed, she wondered? Had Kane picked them up and not mentioned it to Lucas? That didn't sound right.

The first time Kane had touched her, she had sensed an almost child-like sense of honesty in him. Horn dog tendencies aside, he possessed a rare pure heart. She shook her head. No, something else was going on here and she hadn't picked up on it yet.

Leaning forward, she touched the smooth rock with both hands and reached for the Tallan, pulling the energy of the circle inward, giving her the boost she needed to see what others could not. Color and light blended, her vision blurred as she drew the power around her.

A piercing pain struck her in the head as she saw Lara standing in the spot Kira now occupied. Lara's essence invaded her body as she waited, causing nausea to roll through her. As Kira's stomach revolted, Lara began touching the items on the rock.

Her words were mumbled preventing Kira from making out what she chanted. Kira's sight followed Lara's hands to get a closer look and saw three unusual objects: a simple bladed knife with an intricately carved handle, a small black bottle with a cork stopper, and a flat metal disk with a pentacle etched on it.

Tools of a witch.

Unable to decipher what the combination of these three objects were used for, Kira attempted to reach further into Lara's mind. Not everyone with her gift could maneuver this deeply into another mind because it scared them. It was her ability to do it easily and effectively that made her different from most of the other woman in her

Clan and why they considered her even more dangerous during her mating call.

Again, the mind numbing pain in her head struck her, fighting for a stronger hold. Dark images floated across her eyes and she knew then she couldn't maintain the link. The darkness of Lara pulled her towards a painful abyss. She had to pull out fast before she hurt herself.

Pushing away from the dark aura around her, Lara turned and grabbed Kira's arm in a tight vise, locking her inside. She was trapped. The mystery in Lara's glowing eyes beckoned her irresistibly and, when her lips curled into a satisfied smile, Kira's fear and anger knotted inside her. As the pain increased, she wavered, helpless to stop the invasion. Her last thought before succumbing to the darkness was of Lucas. She should have left him a note. *Always have backup.* No truer words had been spoken.

When would she ever trust?

HEARING LARA MOCKING HER WEAKNESS, Kira opened her eyes. "Ah, are you finally going to wake up and play with me? I would have expected someone with your skills and abilities to be more fun, not so weak." Lara glared at Kira as she lay there helpless.

"I thought you were dead," Kira stuttered. She did feel weak and couldn't seem to get her bearings. She sat up and scanned the area around her for a sign of something familiar. Her eyes adjusted to the dark and damp gloom of the cave. Smoke swirled in the room, accompanied by a rancid odor she couldn't identify.

Turning back to Lara, she noticed her pupils were now

black as coal and rimmed in red fire. Lara barely resembled a human woman anymore. In fact she looked more like a creature.

"Dead?" She opened her mouth and roared. "Not hardly. The lot of you are fools to think you can handle me. My revenge has just begun."

"Revenge? For what? Where are we?" The last thing she remembered was getting into Lara's head, but somewhere along the line she'd lost control. Her head still pounded but the adrenalin from fear and anger pushed her forward.

Lara stormed across the cave floor. Her hand swung up, slapping Kira across the face, whipping her head back against a rock wall. The resounding crack reverberated across the cave, shocking Kira from her stupor. She sprang into a crouch and swept her right leg around her body, knocking Lara off her feet and flat on her back. Quickly rising up, Kira slammed her boot against Lara's neck, pinning her to the ground.

"Did you just bitch slap me? Are you kidding me? Enough of your bullshit. What exactly is your fucking problem?" Her anger swelled, as did her power. As Kira lifted her boot to kick Lara in the stomach, she dissolved into a mist. Kira sprang back into a fighting stance and swung around, searching the cave for Lara.

Before Kira could spot her, Lara threw up her hands, throwing two flaming energy balls at her. Kira sprang to her left but not quite fast enough as one of the balls hit her in the thigh. The excruciating pain sizzled down her leg as she slammed into the wall.

The smell of her burning flesh filled the cave along with the sound of Lara's deep chuckle. Images swirled together, a dark haired man standing behind a snarling Lara, the scent of blood and familiar voices faded as Kira slipped into the oblivion of unconsciousness. Damn it. Not again.

AKIRA. Damn it, Kira, answer me.

She heard Lucas in her head, but when she tried to answer him, her brain wouldn't respond. She lay there for a few minutes more, letting her body adjust. Looking around, the swaying trees seemed too peaceful. She realized she was lying next to the same rock where Lara had stood fiddling with her Wiccan weapons.

What the hell had happened and, more importantly, what was that god awful smell? It seemed so familiar. Sitting up, she searched the area for the source. Something on the ground caught her eye. Bending over, she picked up a small vial. There was no label on it so she unscrewed the top, raised it to her nose and took a big sniff. "Eww, that stinks." Rubbing her nose to help rid herself of the foul stench, her vision blurred, sliding her consciousness into a different reality, and it finally dawned on her. "That smells like lavender mixed with something else. Something dark." Like a fog clearing, she realized what was going on. "Holy shit! Black magic." Sweat broke out on her palms and her heart raced faster than it should. Her recent vision revealed not only was Lara not dead, but she had something much bigger planned and she wasn't doing it alone.

Kira, where the fuck are you and why the hell aren't you answering me? Lucas was in her head again.

This time she could have answered him if she wanted, but chose not to. The man in her vision...it had to be him and he was with Lara. He'd been lying to her. Stringing her along. The pain of that realization nearly knocked her down. It all made perfect sense now. The two of them were working together, *He knows he's my mate and, with the help of a black magic witch, he could harvest my powers or at the very least gain control with no trouble at all.*

Not gonna happen. Wondering what her next move should be, she gathered the herbs left on the ground and stuffed them into the empty vial. Slipping the glass bottle into her pants pocket, she turned, crashing into a hard male chest.

Looking up, her body tensed. "Kane, you scared the crap out of me." His face was set in an angry scowl, dark brows furrowed and his mouth in a grim line. She swallowed hard. "What?" She was standing so close to him she could smell him. He smelled like pine and forest.

"Why haven't you been answering Lucas' call?"

She peered around his broad shoulders, expecting to see Lucas walk up behind him. "I know the truth about Lucas."

Kane continued to glare at her as if he could see straight through her. "What truth is that?" Crossing his arms in front of his chest, he waited for her to answer.

"Lucas didn't kill Lara. They faked her death."

"They? What they? Kira, are you feeling okay?" He gently grabbed her shoulders and brought her closer. "I was there, remember? I saw Lucas kill her."

She shook her head, "You're not listening." Kane cupped the back of her head and drew her to his chest. His warmth tempted her. Just for a moment she had second thoughts. After a moment, she shook her head to clear her mind. "No, Lara is a black witch and she and Lucas are trying to take control of me and my powers."

Her worst fears were coming true right in front of her. "Please you have to listen. I had a vision and saw the truth. Lara wants to kill me but Lucas won't let her because he wants the control instead. You have to help me." Lifting her head, she peered into eyes so blue they appeared fathomless, looking for his truth. Would he help her or just turn her over to his brother? Confusion clouded his eyes, giving her a brief moment of hope that he might believe her.

Kira, I know you can hear me, I can feel it. Please, baby, tell me where you are? I just want to help you. Lucas again. No matter how hard she tried, she couldn't block him.

His voice grew stronger in her head the closer he got so she didn't have much time. Kane had to help her or let her go.

How? How could she get him to cooperate?

Kane wrapped his arms around her and stroked up and down her back, comforting her. "Shh. You've been through an ordeal. You're stressed out. He'll be here in a few minutes and then you can straighten all of this out."

His touch sparked a new idea.

She pressed her lips to his, whispering against them. "No. Please. Please help me." He opened his mouth to speak and she thrust her tongue between his parted lips, in a hard and desperate kiss.

Shock rushed through her. She didn't know what she'd expected, but this wasn't it. He wasn't sweet and sunny like she'd expected. He had a darkness that came out spicy and smelling of the earth. An unexpected shiver worked through her.

Heat coursed through her blood, rational thought

disappeared and her mind splintered as she sank into him, completely forgetting about her mission.

She wanted more...more of whatever this was. As a sliver of something dark wound its way around her she suddenly ached for closer contact. To make that happen she threaded her hands through his hair and wrapped one of her legs around him until he was pressed fully against her.

But it still wasn't enough as her mind screamed in equal parts pleasure and terror.

Letting go of his hair, she ripped open her shirt and pressed his work roughened hands to her chest. The rough texture against her smooth, heated skin was intense and almost more than she can handle.

"Lucas," she mumbled against his mouth.

He broke away from her lips then, panting. "Kira, stop. What are you doing? I am *not* Lucas. We can't do this. It's not right." His face wrinkled in concern, but his chest heaved and his body remained pressed against her.

Ignoring his attempt to protest, she fumbled for the zipper on his pants. His words made no sense to her.

"Lucas," she chanted, "Lucas."

Her mind focused on her task. Quickly releasing him, she dropped to her knees.

Grasping her shoulders, Kane pushed her away, making her lose her balance and crash into the dirt on her side.

"No. Stop. Something is very wrong. You belong to Lucas. You are *his* mate."

At his last word, Kira's lucidity momentarily returned, long enough for her to realize what she'd done.

"Oh my God! What the hell? What are we doing?" She scrambled off her knees, backing away from him. "What have you done to me? You're one of them. You trying to control me, too." She grappled with the edges of her blouse, trying to cover herself. She stumbled backwards, desperate now not for touch, but escape.

"Kira, wait."

Not giving him a chance to say more, she turned and ran deeper into the woods. Her inability to understand what was happening around her frightened her more than her mind could take. She grasped her head in her hands, trying to control the throbbing. But it was the pain searing her heart she couldn't handle.

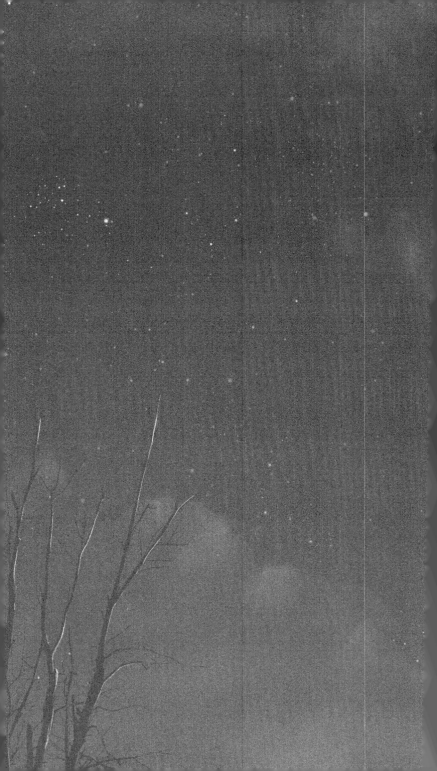

CHAPTER
TWENTY-NINE

ensing Kira's distress, Lucas picked up speed. He'd been trying for hours to talk to her and she refused to answer. His frustration had long ago turned into anger and he couldn't wait to get his hands on her. It was time they had a serious talk. He was her mate, and she couldn't jerk him around like this. They needed to come to an understanding, no matter how temporary.

He didn't know many details about how the mating call affected her kind, but the felines of his clan were restless and desperate to fuck until it was over. Kira seemed far more irrational and his instincts told him he was missing something important.

Bursting into the clearing, he came to a sudden halt at what he saw. His brother standing there in the open with his pants down around his ankles and his dick hanging out.

Growling, Lucas warned Kane of his presence. "What the hell is going on here? Where is Kira? You said you'd found her." Lucas turned around, searching the area for Kira. Her scent was everywhere, including...

Slowly turning back to Kane, he realized just what had been happening here. A murderous red haze flowed through his brain. His heart pumped faster as the anger spread throughout his entire body, leaving him edgy and ready to spring. He could kill Kane for this.

"No, brother, it's not what you think." Lucas stalked closer as Kane grabbed his jeans and fastened them back into place. "Something is wrong with her. She thinks Lara is alive and that you and her are planning to control Kira's powers. And she seemed to be confusing us."

"What?" His body stilled. "That's ridiculous. Where would she get a crazy idea like that?" He raised his eyebrows in question, pointedly looking at Kane. "And what the hell does that have to do with you standing here with your pants down and your dick hanging out?" His eyes narrowed. "Huh?"

Kane stood speechless as the precious seconds ticked by.

Of course he was. What could he possibly say that would make any of this make sense? Hell, he would never understand no matter what happened.

One minute his brother had been helping him find a frightened and skittish Kira and the next...this. Even worse, for a split second when he'd spotted him, Kane had bore the familiar look of pleasure Lucas had seen many times before. He'd been fucking enjoying whatever she did. Lucas wondered if he'd even bothered to try and stop it.

With the undiluted rage rushing through his body, Lucas peeled his lips back in a snarl, revealing razor sharp fangs to his brother. "Cat got your goddamned tongue, little bro?"

Fucking with another shifter's mate under any circumstance got a man killed. And rightly so. Even if he was family.

"Something is seriously wrong, Lucas. She wasn't acting like herself. I've never seen a woman so frantic in my whole life."

"And what about you, brother? Were you acting?" Lucas' voice vibrated with anger as he took another step closer.

"I'm sorry, she took me by surprise. I should have handled the situation better, but it took my brain a few seconds to catch up. However, we'll have to have this out later because I think she needs our help."

Taking a few steps closer, Lucas struck out, punching him straight in the face and sending Kane sprawling across the clearing.

"Stay the fuck away from my mate. I think you've helped enough." Lucas turned back in the direction he'd come and stormed away. He couldn't look at his brother right now, not unless he wanted to live with the guilt of murder for the rest of his life.

The beast in him clawed and fought against his will to do the right thing. He had to leave before he did something he would never be able to take back.

CHAPTER
THIRTY

Winded from running, Kira stopped to catch her breath. She glanced behind her and listened for any telltale sounds of someone following her but heard nothing over her own racing heartbeat. She couldn't afford to stop for long, Lucas or Kane were tracking her. What would they do if they caught her? Kill her? No, she expected Lucas to force her into completing the mating ritual. Just like she had envisioned, he and Lara would tie her down and take what they wanted.

She wouldn't let that happen. She'd make it to Deals Gap before Lucas, Lara, or Kane could catch her. Finding the sheriff would be easy. Getting him to understand her story—a whole other ballgame. She had to try, otherwise Lucas would eventually capture her and she'd be helpless to stop them.

Her training kicked in. She knew these mountains like the back of her hand. She wasn't far from a small creek she could use to mask her tracks as well as her scent. Taking one last look behind her, she turned and took off for the water.

AFTER WHAT FELT like hours of running, the woods thinned and Kira got her first glimpse at the town at the base of the mountain. Deals Gap. Often referred to as the inhospitable section of the southern Appalachians, it was nestled at the mouth of the Dragon.

Home for the strange and supernatural. A small number of humans settled in the area, but for the most part, the Dragon was only occupied by the exiled members of the Clans of MacDonald, Gunn and Comyn.

While all of the Clan members living in this area were direct descendants from the original groups from Scotland that were forced to flee persecution and destined to hide their abilities here in the mountains, these dwellers were the ones who broke the most sacred laws of the Councils.

But they weren't the only ones who wandered through here. Only one road led through the heart of the Dragon and, despite the danger, all walks of life had recently become enamored by the seductive curves of the Dragon.

Reaching the Tree of Shame, Kira sighed. She'd made it. Raking her gaze over the tree, she wondered when would the mortals learn to quit challenging the Dragon? Whenever one lost life or limb, a personal effect of theirs would be added to the tree. Seemed like every time she came through the Gap, the stuff hanging there had multiplied.

Just past the small biker resort next to the tree, she spotted the sheriff's office. Making her way across the road, she attempted to brush away some of the debris on her clothes and straighten her hair.

She needed a shower. Hopefully after she explained what was going on to the sheriff, he'd let her use his facilities to get cleaned up. She'd call her sister or maybe her mom to see about one of them coming to get her. She was going to need to hide for a while.

Pushing open the sheriff's door, she heard the basketball game playing on the radio. She rolled her eyes.

What is it about the human men in these parts and their strange love of basketball?

Spotting the sheriff's boots propped on his desk, her gaze traveled up to his face. Sheriff Dave was a good ten years older than her, but sitting there in his chair lightly snoring, his arms crossed over his chest and his hair hanging over his eyes, he looked ten years younger. Kira let go of the door and let it slam shut.

She smirked as Dave about jumped out of his skin at the bang. "What the hell is going on?" He squinted at her, taking in her appearance. "Uh, ma'am, what happened to you? Was there an accident? Did you have some trouble out on the trails? Are you hurt? You're a mess."

He sprang out of his chair and rushed around the desk. When he got closer he finally recognized her. "Oh my God, Kira, is that you? Here have a seat." He motioned to the couch that ran along the wall parallel to his desk. "Can I get you something? Some water?"

The events of the last few days came crashing down on Kira's shoulders as she started trembling. Shaking violently, she tumbled down onto the offered couch.

Looking at the sheriff, she watched his mouth moving

with words she couldn't hear or comprehend. He ran across the room, jerked open the closet door and retrieved a heavy wool blanket and quickly returned to her side. Placing the blanket around her body, she saw his lips moving again but still couldn't hear what he said.

Her temples pounded in tune with the roar in her ears. Her mind was on overload. She couldn't remember why she'd come. Although she was pretty sure she should be hiding from anyone who knew her. She opened her mouth to speak but only managed a grunt before passing out.

CHAPTER
THIRTY-ONE

L ooking around the tiny cabin, Kira didn't recognize anything. She stood in a one room dwelling with a small cot in the corner, a kitchenette along the back wall, and a dark brown recliner all alone in the middle of the room. Where was she? And more importantly, why was she here?

She strode across the small space and peered out the window to see if she could get her bearings. Instead of analyzing her surroundings, she came face to face with Lucas. His fierce expression upon seeing her in the window startled her. She took three steps back and drew in a gulp of breath.

The door slammed open and he sauntered in. The glower on his face did not bode well for her. He stalked toward her, making her want to turn and run. Instead, she stood her ground.

"What the hell are you doing here?" His angry heat blew across her skin as he glared at her waiting for an answer.

"You brought me here, you big brute, that's how it works." She took a step forward, getting right into his face, daring him to say more.

"How what works? You aren't making any damn sense, woman."

She sighed. She was going to have to explain it all to him. She didn't have much time left and he was her last hope.

"My mating call is controlled by you. Why do you think I fight it so much? Being controlled by a man is the last thing I can stand." She took a step back. Had to. His angry lust called to her and she didn't think she could control herself much longer. She loved him. Needed him to stay alive.

Shoulders slumping, she turned away. For the outcome had already been decided. When she woke again it would be all over. Her conscious self had lost the battle and could no longer see reality.

"I don't give a shit about that. You betrayed me." He didn't yell, he simply spoke. His words ice cold. Remembering what had happened in the last twelve hours, she realized just how lost to her he was.

"You have no idea how much worse this will get. Unless we complete the mating ritual, all is lost for me. I am sorry for what has happened—what will happen."

"Are you crazy? Mating ritual? How can you think of that now? After what you've done?" He turned from her and headed back to the door, leaving her alone as a single tear slid down her face.

"I am sorry, my love," she said. "I should have told you sooner but I just couldn't. Now you must let me go." she whispered the last into his mind but he ignored her and kept going.

"Ms. MacDonald. Ms. MacDonald, wake up." Someone was shaking her awake. Opening her eyes, she found herself staring into the warm, chocolate brown eyes of Sheriff Dave. "Finally, you're awake. I have been tryin' to get you to open those purty eyes of yours for fifteen minutes."

Oh thank God, she was still safe.

She quickly sat up. "Sheriff, I need your help. I'm being followed and it's not safe for me here. One woman has already been killed—well sort of, I think, and I'm supposed to be next."

"Whoa. Whoa. Slow down." He eased down next to her on the couch. "Someone's been killed, you say? That sounds serious. How's about you go back and start at the beginning and tell me what happened. You're not making any sense."

She jumped up and paced. "You don't understand, Sheriff. I don't have much time. I've got to leave here quickly and hide." Her hands shook as she talked. "I watched him kill her with one bite, but now I don't think she's really dead."

"Bite? Are you talking about an animal attack?" He relaxed back against the cushions, clearly relieved.

"No, well yes, uhm—sort of." This wasn't going too well.

"Honey, sit back down here, did you hit your head? I think you might be hurt. You're confused." He patted the couch, beckoning her.

"You don't understand. He's a shapeshifter. A man who turns into a mountain cat. He and his witch Lara want to control my powers. There's a whole clan of shifters living in the Dragon, but this one has gone rogue and wants to hurt me." She was talking so fast trying to get it all out so she could leave. The sheriff just needed to go find him. Lucas might have the supernatural strength of ten men, but tranquilizers or bullets would still take him down

"Kira, sweetheart, why don't you come on over here and lie down? Let me get you something to drink. What about food? Are you hungry? Sometimes low blood sugar can do unusual things to the mind."

While she contemplated his question of food and drink and how he most likely chose not to use the word crazy just then, the door to the sheriff's office swung open and her stepfather strode in.

"What are you doing here?" she demanded. This was a bad sign. She needed to get out now. She backed up a few steps.

"Honey, when you passed out on my sofa I was worried so I called your daddy to come and get you."

Oh great, just what she needed. The sheriff was so gullible. So human. What had she been thinking coming here?

"He's not my daddy," Kira gritted out.

"It's true, Sheriff, I'm just her stepfather." He turned, facing her, his gaze raking over her appearance. "Sheriff, thank you for calling me. You were right, Kira does look ill and in need of her family's care."

Cringing at his words, Kira wondered about her chances of escaping here and not being caught by Lucas. She might rather take her chances with him rather than return to the clan.

"Lawrence, you might want to take her by the doc's office. I think she might have a fever. She seems delirious. Been going on about a man in the Dragon turning into a big cat and attacking her and another woman." He shook his head in disbelief, getting up from the couch. "Quite a tale if you ask me."

Her stepfather's right brow climbed up his forehead before he turned and addressed the Sheriff. "Thanks, Dave, I'll get her back home to her momma and she'll get her fixed right up." Grasping Kira by the arm, harder than he needed to, he led her out of the sheriff's office to the car he'd left running at the curb. The sheriff followed them out and watched them go.

She jerked her arm free and considered a last chance attempt at running away. Where could she go this time? Between Lucas, a witch, her stepfather and a council out to get her, her time had run out. Resigned she slid into the passenger seat of the sleek vintage Cadillac her stepfather adored.

Once inside the car, he chuckled. "Well, Kira, it looks like all that running you did was for nothing. You're right back where you started. Except you've really gotten yourself into a deep hole this time, telling the sheriff Clan secrets. What the hell were you thinking? This is going to require a massive cover up to fix."

"It's not as if he believed them." Not to mention part of her had noticed he actually didn't seem shocked by her supposed lies.

"Doesn't matter, and you know that. It looks like the Council is going to have to take care of you once and for all."

THIRTY-TWO

T hree days later, Lucas emerged from the woods and returned home. As he approached his house, he was thankful no one would be there waiting for him. He wasn't sure he was ready to see Kane yet, but he knew he'd have to face him soon. Something was seriously wrong and had been eating at him for days. Even more so than the scene of his brother in the woods half naked with Kira's scent on him.

The last time he'd seen Kira in his dreams, she'd seemed hopeless and sad. He'd been so angry with her over her betrayal he had refused to listen to what she'd been trying to tell him.

He wished now he had listened. His instincts were screaming at him to find her. She was in some sort of serious trouble. After finally letting go of his stupid pride, he'd tried reaching out to her mind but had found nothing. For whatever reason their link had been severed.

When he slept he dreamt about her continuously, but the dream-walking had ended. He only dreamt of what had been between them. But every time just before he woke, he would hear her plead with him.

Help me. Please.

It really was driving him insane. He needed her so badly. He was in a constant state of arousal and his being in solitude this time had made him miserable. He really needed a good—

"What the hell?" He froze. He'd been wrong. Someone was waiting for him. He considered shifting when he caught the unfamiliar scent of a stranger, but decided to wait. Best to see who it was before he got all grrr on them. While a human was rare this deep into the woods, it was possible.

Lucas opened the door and came face to face with Kane. Not at all what he'd been hoping for.

The banked anger surged forward and it took everything he had to tamp it back down. He swore he would talk this out and save the ass kicking for afterwards.

Kane raised his hands up in surrender. "I know I'm probably the last person you want to see right now, but I have to talk to you. I've been searching for you for two days. Where the hell did you take off to?"

"Probably? Are you kidding me? I definitely don't want to see you right now. Although I guess that's why you threw me off with the new stench. What could be so damned important you have to barge in here right now?" Lucas took a deep breath and let it out slow. He really didn't feel like a fight right now. "Not a good idea to test my patience right now, bro." He stormed through the door, throwing his bag into the corner to deal with later.

"It's Kira."

At the sound of her name coming from Kane's lips, Lucas' blood boiled over and he tackled his brother to the ground. They wrestled around for several minutes before Kane gave in and let Lucas pin him to the floor. With his arm across Kane's neck, Kane had to struggle to talk.

"Damn it, Lucas, give me a chance to tell you what I came for. If it wasn't life or death, I wouldn't be here. I'm not an idiot. I know you need time, but dammit we don't have any more time." Lucas glared at him, watching his face contort in pain, studying his eyes for any sign of deceit. Finally he relented and pushed himself off of his brother.

Kane rubbed his neck. "There's something about Kira you don't know." Lucas flashed a venomous look at his brother. "Just hear me out, I know you want to kill me, but at least let me finish first."

Lucas grappled for control of his anger, but as it abated, the pain in his heart resurfaced making it difficult to look at Kane. Hell, it hurt to breathe.

"Her Council has sentenced her to death. The sentence is to be carried out in less than twenty-four hours."

Lucas abruptly dropped onto the arm of the chair. The pulse in his ears began to roar.

"Why?"

"She has a mental disease that afflicts all of her kind. That's what has been causing her strange episodes. Apparently, once her mating call begins, she has a finite amount of time to complete the mating ritual with a suitable mate before she loses her mind to a complete storm of chaos. When that happens, she becomes totally unstable and her clan's Council issues a death sentence."

"What? Why death?" He was so confused by this. But somehow it fit with their last conversation.

"Apparently, their Council, just like ours, fears exposure to humans and she poses a risk that is unacceptable. They think the only way to control this exposure is to eliminate any and all threats. Even their own kind."

Kane paced now, but Lucas needed to know more. Although he understood vigilance all too well. He'd been forced to carry out sentences in the name of protection. It was an archaic system but one that had worked for centuries.

"Is Kira lost? Has her mind already shut down?" He threw his hands in the air as his mind raced through the possibilities. "Do you know how crazy this sounds? Why the hell didn't she tell me this? I would have saved her." *Probably.* He frowned at his brother. "How the hell do you know all of this anyway?"

Kane hesitated. "Her mother came looking for you two days ago. When Kira was found rambling to the Deal's Gap sheriff about shapeshifters, they collected her and returned home where she was immediately sentenced. Since then, she has been chanting your name. Her Council fears for everyone's safety and had her locked her up until the ceremony."

Fear and panic stabbed at him. "Am I too late? No, don't say it. I don't care what your answer is. I refuse to believe I'm too late to save her." Lucas stood and paced to the door.

"Where the hell is she? And why the fuck didn't I know all about this before? It's my fucking job to know everything about the other Dragon clans," he raged, his heart constricting as if someone had a vise on it. He definitely couldn't breathe.

Lucas grabbed his side table and threw it across the room, smashing it into the door. Panting, he looked back at Kane "Tell me where she is. Now, damn it! I'm going to get her."

Kane turned to the bureau in the hall and fished out a piece of paper from the top drawer.

"What's that?" Lucas impatiently watched his brother unfold the paper and hand it to him.

"This is a map to your mate. Kira's mother came here desperate for me to find you and get you to help her daughter. She said you are the only one who can. Apparently she even in a confused state Kira refuses to mate with anyone other than your dumb ass. So her mother left this for you."

He snatched the paper from his brother and examined the hand scrawled drawings and words. He recognized some of the mountains and caves depicted, but the actual underground cell was an unknown. Obviously her clan had managed to keep this area a pretty good secret from outsiders.

"What about guards? I don't see anything here about them."

"There's a small guard post here." Kane pointed to a small shack on the map about one hundred fifty yards south of the underground holding cells.

"This looks too easy." Lucas rubbed his face and thought long and hard about Kira. Easy or not didn't matter, he would be going for her, but they did need to be smart about this.

"They aren't expecting any trouble. According to her mother, there has never been an incident of escape. So security is at a minimum."

"So they just kill off their unmated women and everyone stands by and watches it happen? That's pretty fucked up." The injustice of it stabbed Lucas like a hot poker. It wasn't the first time one of their council decisions had seemed unjust, but it was the first that affected him so directly.

"This coming from the Guardian who deals death for a group of old men who sit around a table deciding fates based on some ancient laws no one remembers where they even came from."

The bite of Kane's words hit deep and he had to hide the wince behind it. "Point taken." Kane knew he struggled with his orders at times but this was not the time to get into that.

"Whatever. We've got to go now, there isn't much time left." Kane pointed at a duffel bag propped next to the door. I've already packed some essentials."

Lucas nodded, grateful that his brother had known to prepare. Maybe when this was all over he could forgive him after all.

"I'm driving."

THIRTY-THREE

They took the back roads toward MacDonald land as far as the terrain would allow. About a half-mile from the backside of the mountain where the holding cells were located, they were forced to park and leave their Jeep, after hiding it behind a stand of trees and brush. Lucas took a deep breath, filtering through the scents that flooded him until he found the one he was looking for.

"I've got her." He muttered as he removed his clothes and tossed them on the seat. He shifted and ran, knowing he didn't have to worry about Kane—his brother would keep up.

Within minutes they arrived at the underground cell in which Kira was being held. Shifting back into human form, Lucas and Kane cautiously approached the small cave. They had easily slipped past the two-man guard post twenty-five yards back and they were almost there.

The cave had been carved out from the back side of stone mountain. It was also dimly lit, which would make things difficult if they were human. Before they got around the first bend, Lucas scented the unmistakable fear coming from Kira.

His stomach heaved at the thought of her suffering. Unable to stand it, he sprinted past the line of cells to the farthest one where they had his mate locked up, ignoring the warning hiss of his brother.

Lucas made it to the cage undetected but stopped short when he heard the noises coming from inside.

Lucaaaassss. Lucaaaassss. Lucaaaassss. Hearing Kira chant his name stopped him cold. She sounded like a feral cat. He should know. He'd been responsible for putting down enough of them when they were past the point of no return. Would he be able to bring her back from this?

He had to. He refused to believe they ended like this.

The lock on the door was no match for his strength and easily gave way when he pulled on it. He eased the door open slowly so as to not frighten her when a sense of deja vu washed over him.

Crouched in the corner, she didn't notice him walk in. He approached her like he would a frightened animal while speaking softly. "Kira. Kira, honey, it's me. Lucas."

At the sound of his voice she started shrieking at the top of her lungs. In the cave the sound amplified against the stone walls and would surely carry straight to the guardhouse.

Lucas flew to her side, grabbed her body up against his and covered her mouth to stop the screams. She blindly fought him, scratching at his arms, kicking her legs, all in her wild attempt to get loose. While her strength shocked him, he still held her with ease.

Kane came running in. "What the hell is going on in here? Everyone is going to hear her screeching. Are you trying to get us killed?"

She continued screaming against his hand as well as jerking her body like a wild banshee to get away.

"I don't think she recognizes me. She's scared to death and frantic to get free. If her goddamn pulse is any indication, she's about to have a fucking heart attack."

Kane took a step back and peered down the cave tunnel. "We're never going to get her out of here like this. Lucas, you're going to have to perform the mating ritual right here, right now. It's our only hope." He pointed at Kira. "Her only hope."

"And how do you suppose I'm going to do that with her kicking and screaming? We don't have the time or equipment to tie her up and gag her."

Kane didn't answer him right away and he looked up at him. His brother didn't say a word, but Lucas knew exactly what he thought.

"Uh, no don't even go there. It's not going to work."

"We have to do something. You have any better ideas to calm her down long enough for you to do the nasty and bite the damn mark at the same time?"

Lucas struggled with a solution. An alternative to what his brother suggested. But he had to do something and do something quick. Kane's ill-spoken suggestion made the animal inside snarl. He wanted his brother's blood for even thinking oh her in that way. But if they didn't get out of here soon, they'd be discovered and he didn't think her Council's reaction to his interference would go in his favor.

Lucas bent his head in resignation. "Fine. Get over here

and help me hold her down." He looked up and met his brother's gaze. "Whatever it takes to save her."

For a moment the air around them sizzled. Despite the tension, he'd find a way to hold the animal back long enough for his brother to help. He hoped. The idea of his brother touching her in any capacity already had his stomach roiling.

Lucas shifted so Kira's back was up against the front of his body, one arm wrapped around her waist the other covering her mouth tightly. "I can't let go or she'll alert the whole damn clan with her screams."

Kane walked in front of her and tried talking to her, trying to soothe her fears while Lucas did the same at her ear. No amount of sweet talk or petting seemed to make much of a difference. Until his finger brushed across her nipple.

She continued to wiggle and squirm but her screams behind his hand were beginning to change.

"She may not be sure who we are, Lucas, but I can—uh—smell her—."

"Shut the fuck up!" His words were barely legible through his locked jaw and gritted teeth.

"Just keep going. What you're doing is having a definite effect."

A fierce growl rumbled in his chest. The more words that came from his brother's mouth, the less he wanted to go through with this. Not with the red haze of murderous rage clouding his vision.

Kane held up his hands in surrender. "I'm just saying."

Lucas forced himself to relax, the mating messed a

little with his own control as well. The beast inside was as torn between destruction and taking as he was.

And deep down, where it mattered the most, he knew he could trust his brother.

"Her arousal is having an effect all right. An effect on me. I don't want to hurt her." His full erection pressed firmly against the top of her buttocks. The more she wriggled and fought with him, the harder he became.

Circumstances be damned, he needed her. Maybe more than she needed him. It had to be now.

First though, she needed to stop making so much damned noise.

If he couldn't tell her how he was feeling he'd have to show her. "I can't believe I'm going to say this, but I think we are going to have to do this together."

Kane stared at him, uncertainty written all over his face.

"Are you crazy? I don't need my throat ripped out today." Kane mumbled, backing up a few steps.

"I don't have a fucking choice here now do I?" Lucas hissed. "We don't have much more time here and I'm going to have to let go of her to complete the ritual. Besides, it's not as if we haven't done this before."

"Yeah, but I don't recall a single time before her when my life was in danger because I had my hands on a woman. This will make you want to kill me all over again when this is over. Nope. No thanks." He held up his hands and moved away.

They didn't have time for this. He knew his brother was pushing him for some sort of promise, so he swallowed his pride and proceeded to beg. "Please, brother, help me save my mate." The look in Kane's eyes shifted immediately. He knew he wouldn't have to ask again.

Kane wasted no time and quickly moved to Kira, pressing his body up against hers. She was now sandwiched tightly between the two men, which hampered her efforts at getting loose. Lucas used all of his strength to contain and quiet her while Kane started a slow and easy seduction.

"No shifting," Kane said. "I don't trust your cougar not to kill me for this."

Lucas nodded his head. "Agreed." They both knew this wasn't going to be easy. He absolutely preferred his mate as far away from his brother as possible.

Threading his hands through her hair to hold her still, Kane brought his lips down to her neck, and with soft whispers and light kisses he worked to sooth whatever frightened her.

Several minutes later he sighed a small relief when Kira's natural instincts to mate pushed through and her attempts to scream against his hand turned into whimpers of need.

She still struggled, but he didn't think it was as much about getting away as it was getting closer now. What with her ass rubbing up and down his dick being a clear sign. By no small miracle, he maintained a tight grip and brought his own lips down on the back of her neck.

Despite her loss of full control, the mating call emerged superior, driving her toward him instead of away. Soon she would be lost to it and it wouldn't cease until her mate completed the ritual.

Him.

He was her only chance. His heart clutched. What would they do if she survived tonight? Would she ever believe his true feelings? That he saw her as far more than a duty.

He forced that fear from his mind. It did neither of them any good to think of that right now. He had to save her. At whatever cost. Her life was more important than her anger.

Counting on his brother to keep a level head during the process, Lucas gave in to the need and savored the unique sweet taste of her skin. How he had missed that. He nuzzled and nibbled until Kira writhed in his arms.

Her sudden gasp under his fingers had him looking over her shoulder, where he saw Kane had wrapped his fingers around her slender arms and locked them against his thighs so she couldn't move.

Despite his reluctance to admit it, he was on some level grateful to Kane and his willingness to risk his life for her. Jokes and fights aside, family was still family and they were apparently still willing to come together for each other.

Now to get his mate to come around.

Lucas tuned out his brother and trailed his tongue along the contours of her back, she showed her appreciation by once again wiggling her jean-clad ass against his barely contained erection. "Kane, take off her pants. I need to touch her."

He brother moved fast while maintaining his hold on her with one hand. He made quick work of his task, practically shredding the denim from her body with his claws.

Lucas slid his hand down the smooth expanse of her

belly, diving right into her tight red curls, seeking her clit. She was ready for him. So wet. He wished he had time to get down on his knees, spread her legs and lap up every drop of her.

Such a shame for all that sweetness to go to waste, but there'd be time to make up for it later.

If she forgave him.

She was about to become his mate. A fact neither of them took lightly. His breath hitched at the thought and his cock was near to bursting. The cat snarled for him to hurry. He would have to make this up to her when she recovered. He'd show her with every touch how much she meant to him. It would work. It had to.

Kira thrashed around in both of their arms, not because she wanted to get away but in a renewed and obvious desperation to be fucked.

He removed his hand from her mouth, releasing her moans, which were almost as loud as her screams.

"For Goddess' sake do something to quiet her down." He glared at Kane, making it clear he was desperate.

For once Kane was smart and Lucas saw nothing but concern in his brother's eyes as he pulled her forward and buried her head in his chest. In that position he knew they were locked together unless she was released.

"Hurry up before she does something we'll all regret —" Kane hissed.

Her head was practically in his lap and her movements put her in the position to rub again Kane's lap. In a momentary laps, he growled, forcing his brother's attention to him.

"I tried to tell you this was a bad idea. So fucking get on with it."

Watching Kira move against Kane nearly made his head explode as he fought back the urge to shift and attack. He fought for a breath and held it as long as he could until some of the anger eased.

He had to focus on the mating. Instead of attacking, Lucas closed his eyes, fisted his throbbing length and imagined those lush lips of hers wrapped around him again.

He also worked his fingers with more pressure against her clit, keeping her attention on him as best he could. "That's it baby, ride my fucking fingers. Focus on how good this feels and listen to my voice. Let me make you come."

Kane's savage hiss almost drew him back from the moment, but when he opened his eyes all he saw was Kira bent over with her ass up in the perfect position for him to take her. Grasping her hips, he lined up the head of his cock to her entrance. He wanted to stop and savor this moment, but knew there wasn't time.

He sighed. "Next time, baby. I promise."

Without further hesitation, he drove himself into her in one hard thrust. She screamed around Kane's hold, who did something he couldn't see to tighten his hold and smother the sound.

Fuuccckkk.

She was so snug around him it was hard for him to think. Her strong, silken walls caressed and pulled all at the same time. She was beyond perfect for him.

"Mine. Mine. Mine," Lucas chanted as he pounded into her repeatedly. With no time to prolong this incredible moment, he reached between their bodies and pinched her bud, thrusting her into a release that squeezed him tighter than a fist.

Kane grunted. "I can't hold her much longer. She's fucking strong."

Lucas smiled, but ignored his brother's concern. Kane would do whatever it took for him to finish the ritual. This was his mate. The woman he wanted to cherish forever. The one he'd sacrifice anything for if it meant she continued to live.

Anything for her.

As Kira's body squeezed him through her orgasm, he felt time rushing past. Goddess, she was it. All he'd thought about for days was how much he missed her next to him, her mouth on his skin or her body wrapped around his.

Maybe she would argue he only wanted her because of the mating call or because the sex turned lava hot between them, but he didn't think like that at all.

Nature created lust and desire for each other, but caring about her and falling in love with her couldn't be created through fate.

Either way their momentous moment had arrived. He lifted her hair and exposed her mark. On automatic pilot his body blanketed her back until he could swirl his tongue around that little spot of magic that flamed with their heat.

"So beautiful," he panted at her ear.

Kane cursed on a groan. "Fucker. I hate you."

Her inner muscles squeezed around Lucas. It was too much. This was it. He had to complete the ritual now.

Once they mated like this it fused a bond for life. All manner of choice for his future would be gone. His independence lost forever. She would be his everything and him hers.

The thought she might hate him for this made his heart ache. The consequences of their mating made his head spin, but one truth was more important than any other...

She would die without this and he would not let her die.

Mine. To love and protect.

Unwilling and unable to hold back another second, he thrust his canines into the mark, breaking the skin as his release blasted into her womb.

The pleasure intensified ten fold. His legs wobbled, nearly tumbling them to the floor. Kira's passion laced whimpers rose fiercely and then almost as quickly faded as her body went limp and she passed into unconsciousness.

Good Goddess, her skin under his lips was so hot he thought it might melt. He jerked against the heat, the burn searing him from the inside out, but his mouth remained locked to her skin.

Strange images of Kira appeared in his mind. Kira as a child, hiding in the woods. As a teen, exploring her new woman's body. Kira as she was now, running in the woods, scared for her life.

Lucas' mouth flooded with the bitter taste of her fear. Finally, she appeared very much like now but with skin that glowed and her belly swollen with a child. Tasting the sweetness of the love she felt, he was shocked to also find the sour taste of her sadness. His heart stuttered.

The utter desolation of her pain filled his head as mind numbing confusion wrapped around him like a heavy wet blanket.

Oh, hell. What had they done?

When her flesh cooled, his mouth popped free, releasing his canines as he slid free. Lucas gently laid Kira down on the ground. Dressing quickly, he glanced around the room for Kane. He hadn't gone far. He'd simply moved to the doorway, his back turned to them.

"Kane, help me get her ready to go." They needed to hurry and get back to his cabin. While the mating was complete and her clan could do nothing about that, he wasn't sure they would accept the trespassing onto their sacred land. Not to mention his own clan might see fit to punish him for his actions.

Yeah, his own Council. Tonight he'd broken damn near every rule he'd been raised to protect. How many people had he banished for less than this? Including his older brother Malcolm...

Malcolm. His brother's angry face the last time he'd seen him hovered in his conscious. He'd vowed the clan would regret pushing him out.

"Holy shit! Why didn't it come to me sooner?" Banishing Mal had been the worst thing he'd ever had to do as Guardian. The guilt had eaten at him for months, nearly driving him to leave the clan himself.

It had been five long years since that fateful day. Some of the pain and guilt of loss had faded but Malcolm had not been forgotten or forgiven.

"Lucas, what the hell are you talking about? We've got to go." Kane demanded.

"It's Mal. The entire time I was held prisoner there had been a subtle but familiar scent I couldn't place." Lucas scrubbed his face with his hands. "I hadn't been sure about Lara or her motives and had pretty much concluded she had an accomplice. I could tell someone was masking, but every time that bitch got too close I would get the tiniest hint of a smell I couldn't quite place until now. Now I know." His voice dropped dangerously low. "He's the one responsible for my capture. It has to be. Who else would know how to get near us?"

"C'mon, Lucas. There has to be another explanation. Malcolm is an asshole but you really think he would kidnap you? Why? What would he have to gain?"

Kane was right. It didn't make sense yet. But it didn't have to. His instincts were spot on. "I don't know all the details yet but I'm positive it was him. And that means that my mate's near death adventure with that witch Lara rests squarely on our brother's shoulders."

THIRTY-FOUR

Kira came awake with a parched throat and an aching body. She groaned and rolled to her side. *What the hell happened?*

Reluctant but curious, she opened her eyes and stared at the space in front of her. In all of two seconds she recognized Lucas' bedroom. Although how she'd gotten here she had no idea. Releasing a long breath, she rolled back over and stared at the ceiling. Part of her wanted to jump up and investigate and the other part didn't care anymore. If she was dreaming again then so be it.

The seconds ticked by in her head and nothing happened. No voices, no angry alpha standing over her ready to ream her up one side and down the other. If she wanted to know how she'd gotten here she'd have to find out on her own. Kira attempted to sit up but halted when a piercing pain stabbed through her shoulder. Puzzled, she reached to rub the spot and came in contact with a bandaged wound.

Struggling, she stood and walked across the room to

the mirror attached to the bureau. A sick feeling in the pit of her stomach warned her she might not be ready to face what she would see. Too bad she never listened. She peeled the tape from her skin and gently lifted the white gauze, crying out when her worst fears were realized. There were two puncture marks in the middle of her mating mark.

Oh, God. No!

Kira called to the Tallan to help her remember what had happened. She fell to her knees as vivid and detailed memories flooded her brain. Images of her being screwed by Lucas while Kane held her still and of Lucas biting her while she whimpered for more crowded her mind.

She'd been completely out of control when they found her, unable to function in a normal capacity. Her body had demanded the mating from Lucas. Instincts had taken over and she'd been given the greatest ecstasy of her life. When Lucas' canines pierced the mark, her body had exploded in pleasure like nothing she had ever experienced before.

The overload of sensations had splintered her body and soul, every nerve ending rippling in bliss. The orgasm had washed over them with shocking intensity. Even now, electricity from that joining still coursed through her veins. Her sex heated and swelled at the memories, preparing her for another wild bout with her mate.

Her body. The betrayer. Every scheme and idea she'd worked on had failed. She now belonged to a man.

Speaking of betrayal, where the hell is Lucas?

She reached for his touch and found him close by on the front porch, sweat pouring off of him.

His mind swirled with angry emotions as he repeatedly

punched the hell out of his heavy bag. She started to push further and stopped.

No, she wasn't quite ready to see the hatred that must surely burn there. He'd somehow found out about her situation and saved her life. Now his regret would kill her.

Unfortunately for her, she remembered everything she had said and done when her mind broke down. What she had done in the woods to Kane, the secrets she had spilled to the sheriff, even the unfounded fear she had experienced from Lara's death. She had betrayed her kind. And more importantly, she had betrayed Lucas.

Sweat beaded on her clammy skin as the stress and tension of the last few days tried to escape. Hands trembling, she pushed against the floor trying to get off of her knees. She gripped the edge of the short bureau and hauled herself back up.

Damned if she wasn't going to pull herself together and face him. Lucas had mated them and now they were stuck. Ironically, she was now mated to the man she loved. Yes, she could finally admit she had fallen in love with him. How could she not?

Besides the sexual chemistry they shared, she'd fallen for his unwavering devotion to his family and clan, the fact his intelligence rivaled her own, and in some quirky way, his tendency to want her out of harms way charmed her.

Unfortunately for her, he would never love her back. She'd gone *waaay* too far. And now her powers were linked to his will. The one thing she had feared the most.

Wiping away the lone tear that threatened to fall, she stood up tall and stiffened her spine. She had to face him, find out what his intentions were regarding her. If he thought to use her for her powers, well, he had another thing coming. If her abilities were now incomplete without him, so be it. She couldn't live out the rest of her extended life with a man who didn't love her. She had sworn to not be weak like her mother. There was still such a thing as free will. She hoped.

If not, then unlike her mother, she wasn't afraid to end her own life in order to stop another madman.

Checking her reflection in the mirror, she smoothed her hair, straightened her shoulders and declared herself ready. She might look a bit pale but she was more than ready to take on one overgrown house cat.

She yanked the door open and skidded to a stop. Lucas stood there, waiting.

"Going somewhere, darling?" he sneered. He must have been listening to her thoughts because he looked pissed off. Pissed, but damn gorgeous. Her eyes raked over his body. His chest was gloriously bare and covered with a light sheen of sweat from his workout. The golden, sun browned skin was covered by that layer of fine hair that she knew would tickle her nipples when she rubbed up against him. That fur alone had the power to make her forget everything else and do nothing but sexy, dirty things to her man.

As if that wasn't enough, his workout pants were loosely fastened and rode dangerously low on his hips. So low in fact, the curve of his groin muscle distracted her. A soft, betraying moan came from her throat and her fingers itched to reach out and pull the flimsy string that held his pants up. She wanted to see more of his glorious body.

Saliva pooled in her mouth. She yanked her head back

up, shaking it back and forth, forcing herself to look away to keep from drooling all over the place. She needed to get a grip. They would get nowhere if she couldn't stop thinking about licking him from head to toe. *Ugh.*

A deep chuckle rumbled from his chest. "Are you planning to eat me alive?" His smart ass attitude was as effective as if he'd dumped a glass of ice water over her head.

"I was on my way to find you. To demand some answers."

His eyes hardened like chips of ice and, just like that, the easy laugh disappeared.

Fine, it would be easier for her if he stayed cold and distant. Just seeing him like this made her want to drag him down to the floor and grind her body on his. She didn't know much about riding him bronc style, but how hard could it be to learn?

"You sound a little tart for a woman who just woke up from one hell of a destructive bender."

She winced at his not so subtle accusations. He had every right to be angry with her. She should have just told him what was happening to her. Instead, her pride had demanded her silence and now she would pay the steep price.

"Why, Lucas? Why would you mate with me after everything I've done? Was it some sort of warped sense of obligation to save me? That's exactly what I didn't want to happen. Knowing you felt sorry for me enough to sacrifice yourself makes me sick." The acid in her stomach came to life, making her statement a churning reality. "I need to get away from here and get back to my real life." She knew it was the right thing to do, even if she had to pay for the sacrifice everyday for the rest of her life.

"Not without me you don't."

Her head jerked up. "Excuse me?"

"Damn, woman, you are the most stubborn female I have ever met. Were you going to let me get a word in during that tirade?"

She opened her mouth, about to fire off a retort but his hand came up and pressed against her lips. "My turn, Kira."

Whatever. He could take his best shot. She nodded.

"It's true that I couldn't bear to let you die that way. What kind of person would I be if I did?"

Emotion clogged her throat at his words. He was a warrior just like her, and to people like them, sacrifice would never be too high a price for another's life.

"Don't you get it? You're *my* mate just as much as I am yours." He grasped her shoulders and pulled her up against his chest. "Do you even understand the implications of mating with a shapeshifter? There are good reasons why we don't mate very often."

As confusion bloomed inside her, he crushed her mouth with his lips. Spearing his tongue into her mouth, she could taste his anger and frustration along with his healthy lust. "It's impossible for you to leave me now, or I you. We can no longer survive without each other. At least not well. The longing would drive us or maybe just me, mad."

She couldn't really process what he said while he stroked her skin. His rough hands abrading across her flesh sent shivers down her back. Her senses heated up and she wanted nothing more than to lie back and beg him for more.

What had she been about to say? She couldn't remember. Couldn't think. Only wanted more. Rubbing her hands up his chest, she flicked his flat nipples lightly. His sharp intake of breath was a glorious reward and she flicked them again. He growled and bit her lip. The pleasure/pain sensation shot straight to her core as her juices flowed to her thighs.

Moving over to Lucas' ear, she showered him with soft kisses before biting down. She didn't know what was with all of the biting, but it felt good and right. The two of them panted and their hearts raced in beat together. She didn't care. Her only thought was of fucking. She needed him and needed him now. Dropping to her knees, she pulled the damn string that taunted her earlier and pulled the sweatpants from his body. His erection bounced up and against his belly, before rebounding right against her lips. She flicked out her tongue and captured it to her.

He growled again. "Yes, baby. Put it between those lush lips of yours. I need you to suck it so bad." His words heightened her need even further as she wrapped her hands around his shaft, guiding his erection to her eager mouth. The satiny smooth head pulsed against her. Oh, she wanted more. She hungrily engulfed his entire length, caressing the sensitive underside with her tongue. His skin tasted of salt and spice. Delicious.

It still wasn't enough. Her sex pulsed, aching for touch. She released one hand from his erection and slid her hands inside her own shorts in search of her pulsing need.

"Yes, baby, that's perfect. Suck me while I watch you

touch yourself. Show me how much you need me." He fisted her hair and fucked deeper into her mouth. His hips began a nice, even thrusting as her fingers stroked her clit with the same rapid rhythm.

He rocked faster. "Kira, it's too good. You're going to make me come." She sucked harder—wanting it, begging for it. After a few more shallow thrusts, he pulled from her suckling mouth. She mewled in protest.

"No, baby, I'm not coming yet. I have to taste you. Your new scent is about to make me fucking crazy."

"New scent?"

"Oh, yeah. You're marked now and every cat around will know it. You carry my scent as well as yours. It calls to me." Flipping her onto her back, right there on the soft throw rug, he spread her legs wide and stared down at her. "Look at you, so beautiful and hot. Making me crazy with need."

Slowly, way too slowly, he licked her slit from her opening straight up to her protruding sensitive knot of nerves.

"God, Lucas, you're torturing me." She tried to wiggle harder against his tongue but his hands held her legs tight enough to keep her in place. He wasn't about to give her the control she so desperately wanted.

Her need began to border on pain as he delved one finger inside her. More. She wanted more. She wanted him to fill her and make her scream. She grabbed his hair and pulled hard. "Lucas, if you don't fuck me right this second I am going to kick your ass!" In retaliation for her outburst, he bit at her sensitive nub and added a second finger to the first, further stretching her tight channel. Her eyes rolled back in her head.

"Maybe that's just what you need, sweetheart. A little ass whipping. And I'm just the man to give it to you." Withdrawing his fingers from her clenching sex, he flipped her onto her stomach and pulled her up onto her knees. Before she even had a chance to respond, she received a hard, stinging smack right on her ass.

Too stunned by his actions to speak, her body flamed from the pleasurable sting. With each subsequent blow, the heat made her nerves pulse harder. "Lucas, please I need you so bad," she begged. She couldn't help it. Her body was in control, not her mind. The only thing she wanted was him filling her right now. She reached for her aching flesh, desperate for relief, but he pushed her hand away.

"No, only I get to touch it now." He smacked her ass again, simultaneously filling her sex with his hard, thick length.

She screamed out. Oh God. The stinging of her ass combined with him stretching her blew her mind. Her body shook.

Before she could take another breath, his hands grabbed her cheeks and spread them wide.

"Kira, I'm going to take you here, too, baby." The words were spoken as a given not a choice. No one had ever taken her that way, but here in this moment she didn't care. Caution and worry were gone, replaced by a driving, frenzied need as she pushed harder against him, striving for deeper penetration. She belonged to Lucas heart and soul and would give him whatever he wanted.

"Yes, Lucas—" Before she finished her plea for more, he pressed the tip of his finger into the ultra tight hole. Dark spots waved in her vision as she instinctively pushed back driving both his hard cock and long finger deep inside her. The intense sensations sizzled through her blood as her muscles clenched around him in an explosive and unstoppable release.

He roared his satisfaction, pumping hard inside her body. He added a second finger to her ass, further stretching her opening. Just when she was sure he was nearing his orgasm, he pulled completely from her body. The shock of his sudden departure made her legs tremble, too weak to look back to see what he was doing.

But she didn't need to see, she knew what was coming.

His fingers delved into her, dipping in and out and covering them with her juices. Like in her dreams, those fingers moved up to her ass, pushing into the tight hole and rubbing them around.

He was lubricating her. Preparing her for his cock. She shuddered, somewhat frightened by how much she wanted it.

Then he was at the opening, prodding her to open and then pushing past her tight ring of muscles, forcing it gently in. Her body tensed when it started to burn, a soft cry escaping her lips.

"Relax, Kira, trust me, baby. It will hurt less if you relax. In a minute you're going to be so surprised." As he pushed ruthlessly inside, he sparked against unexplored pleasure points. He pressed further and the combination of pleasure and pain threatened to throw her headlong into another abyss.

Finally seated, he bent across her backside whispering into her ear. "Do not come, Kira. Not until I say so. Do you hear me? A little delayed release is going to make this even better." Her heart raced and her body shook as she tried to control the flash of heat building within. "Kira?"

"Yes, okay, I'm trying." Her words were breathless from the struggle.

"If you come before I say so, I'll be forced to punish you and start all over again." She didn't have time to heed his warning. He slowly pulled back, swamping her with a dark pleasure that burned out of control.

"Oh God, Lucas, it's too much, I—I can't take it." Sweat beaded on her body as she continued the fight, holding back the explosion.

"No! Not yet." Lucas slammed in and out of her ass harder, forcing her orgasm to the surface.

"Please—please," she begged. Her words died as she lost the fight for control.

"Come now, mate."

One more drag and her body splintered, flying apart. Her screams filled the room, long and loud. The climax hit her so hard and strong all she heard was the blood roaring in her head.

"Yes, baby. You're mine now, Kira. I'm coming." Heat flooded her backside, pushing her farther than she thought possible. More screams filled the room.

Time passed as they bucked and thrashed against each other, unable to quell the sensations. Pleasure, warmth, and most of all love flowed between them as their bodies stilled.

Lucas collapsed over her as he slipped from her. He

mumbled something to her but she didn't hear what he said. He'd worn her out, and she needed more sleep. Her last thought before succumbing was despite everything she had put him through she couldn't give him up. He belonged to her now.

CHAPTER
THIRTY-FIVE

While Kira lay sleeping, Lucas caressed her hip, marveling at the beauty of her shape. It still amazed him how every curve of her body fit perfect against his.

She'd passed out after sex and he worried if he'd gone too far with her. He couldn't bear it if she looked at him differently when she woke. Still possessed by anger, he'd wanted to claim her in his own way as well as punish her for what she'd done to him. Would she understand that had soothed his soul as well as satisfied the cat?

She'd been incredible. Not only had she submitted to his darker desires and needs, she'd embraced them with a wanton desire of her own.

Instead of trying to stop his invasion, she had prodded him to succumb to his aggressive nature. Remembering her fervent responses, his body stirred to life again. Unbelievably, he wanted to roll her over and take her again.

Shaking his head to clear his mind, he gently got up from the bed. This time he'd go out for a run instead.

Shifting would free his mind of his problems, giving him a clear shot at deciding the best course of action from here.

Despite everything they had been through together, she still thought to leave him. Maybe he'd just tie her to the bedposts and sexually torment her until she admitted she had feelings for him.

She won't leave me. I won't allow it. Satisfied that they'd work it out, he left the room with quite the wicked grin spreading across his face.

THE CRISP MOUNTAIN AIR RUFFLED LUCAS' fur as he sprang across the stream. The freedom and power he experienced in his animal form exhilarated him. Due to the harsh terrain of the Dragon, there were few humans who ventured off the nearby mountain road, leaving Lucas and his clan free to roam the land as they saw fit. It was rare anyone from outside his clan tried to harm any of them. But occasionally one of their kind would be spotted and reported, but with no evidence it got chalked up to the smaller native bobcat.

Mountain lions, cougars and panthers were all considered extinct east of the Mississippi except in a small region of Florida. Little did they know. The other two clans living in the Dragon, while only separated by a few miles from each other, kept to themselves as much as possible. Although the wolves had a thing for stirring up trouble.

In the two decades Lucas had served his clan as Guardian, only a handful of its members had tried to break the laws and mate outside. All who did were banished.

Once gone from the clan, their psychic powers would diminish until after about three years they would completely disappear. Leaving them to live out the rest of their extended lives as humans.

Just like—

Lucas stopped in his tracks. The wind carried a familiar scent to his nostrils. One he hadn't scented in these woods in a very long time. A low growl reverberated in his chest. Adrenalin coursed through his veins and his hair stood on end. Snarling, he turned to face the intruder.

"Hello, Lucas." The man chuckled, a harsh sound that didn't come across as humor at all. "Surprised to see me?"

Lucas quickly shifted back to human form. Startled confusion gave way to white hot anger as he looked upon his older brother, Malcolm, for the first time in five long years.

"What the hell are you doing here? You know I have the authority to kill you no questions asked for returning here without permission," he spat.

"Careful, brother. Considering what you've been up to the past twenty-four hours, I don't think you've got the right to judge me any longer. You've become quite the rule breaker."

Shit, he was right. Mating with Kira was just as bad as Malcolm's crimes, at least according to the Council. In Lucas' eyes there were shades of gray not simply black and white.

Still, he and Kira weren't going to be risking clan exposure to mortals anytime soon. Unlike Malcolm, they honored those rules and traditions and were willing to put their lives on the line for those beliefs.

"What do you hope to accomplish by coming here today? Haven't you done enough damage already?" Lucas had no evidence that Mal was responsible for his kidnapping, but his showing up here seemed like questionable timing at best and he wasn't sure how to handle it.

"I want my abilities back. No longer being able to shift has long term repercussions I don't think anyone here was aware of. Unless of course you've turned into a sadist bastard who enjoys seeing others suffer."

Lucas snorted. "Fancy talk from someone always working his next scheme no matter who suffers for it. Besides, you look perfectly healthy to me." In fact he looked remarkably just like the day he had left the Dragon. Big, strong, and cocky.

"You don't get it do you?"

"What the hell are you talking about, Mal? We didn't do anything to your abilities. There's no psychic link anymore, big deal. You don't need telepathic power to live out a normal life."

For some weird reason, that made Malcolm laugh. An evil sound that scraped along his spine, but a laugh nonetheless. "Still a blind slave to the Council, huh? Guess you're never going to learn."

Malcolm's mocking tone raked over his skin. Lucas' arm shot out and grasped Malcolm by the neck, choking him. Mal grabbed his hand but didn't pull himself free.

"What's wrong, Mal, Cat got your tongue?" His brother had some nerve showing up here and insulting him. Lucas was spoiling for a fight and as far as he was concerned, Malcolm had arrived just in time to give him one. "Have you come to try and take the big bad Guardian down? Fine. Let's go."

Still Malcolm didn't pull free from Lucas' grasp. He was pulling at Lucas' hand but not hard enough to break free.

"I—I can't. You're choking me." Malcolm's face turned a nice shade of red as if he actually struggled from Lucas' grip.

Lucas let go of Malcolm and turned his back, walking away. His brother had changed and it wasn't for the better. Malcolm disgusted him.

"Lucas, for God's sake, listen to what I am telling you. My animal strength is gone, I can't shift anymore and I think I might be dying."

Lucas stopped dead in his tracks. That made no sense.

"Don't bullshit me, Mal. What do you *really* want?" he replied in a low, frustrated voice. He'd had enough with the lies. And as much as he wanted to make Malcolm suffer for everything he'd done, he couldn't bring himself to do it. The family bond between them ran deeper than he cared to admit.

"Look, I need your help. You can help me get back what I've lost and in return I will help you save your mate. But we have to hurry or it'll be too late."

Lucas' blood ran cold at the distinct scent of truth coming out of his brother's mouth. "What have you done?"

Malcolm shook his head. "This time it's not me, I swear. There is another. And apparently your mate is quite valuable to him."

THIRTY-SIX

K ira leaned back in her chair, relaxing and soaking up the sun. She had awoken to an empty cabin *again* and, after a quick shower, decided she needed some fresh air.

Mulling over all the events of the last few days, Kira couldn't believe that she was mated and in love. What a mess she'd gotten herself into. What had Lucas meant about what happens when his race mates? Would something happen to either of them when she went home? When she left, would she be able to adjust to the loss of her powers?

So wrapped up in her own personal demons, Kira failed to sense someone approaching until a deck board creak behind her.

She twisted around and found Lara looming over her. The smile sitting on the woman's face twisted Kira's stomach into knots. Before she was able to say or do anything, Lara flung an energy ball straight for Kira's head.

Fighting panic, Kira dove to the ground, barely evading

the deadly strike. Her heart raced. Fortunately, she'd been trained to handle this kind of attack and instinctively went into offensive mode. Kira mentally pushed Lara across the deck into the rear wall of the cabin, momentarily knocking the wind out of the other woman.

"What exactly is your fucking problem? You're supposed to be dead and this is getting so old." She was sick and tired of this witch popping up to cause trouble over and over. "What do you want from me?" Her jaw clenched, her eyes narrowed slightly as she stared down at the prone witch.

"I don't care one way or another about you. I have a job to complete here and you happen to fall smack in the middle. Then at least one of the Gunn Guardians can pay for what they did to me."

Her lips were twisted in a nasty, angry snarl, but something else wavered in her eyes for a split second. Sadness maybe? As quickly as it came it disappeared. Replaced by the blood red color of rage.

"What exactly did they do to you? And what does it have to do with me?" Kira scanned the surrounding area for her options. The deck was flat and open but if she could make it to the ground without being blown to pieces she could take cover in the tree line surrounding the cabin.

Before she got a chance to make a run for it, three more energy balls whizzed by her head.

Fuck! So close!

Lucas I hope you can hear me. The witch is back and one way or another this bitch is going down. Just as soon as I shove one of those energy balls down her goddamn throat.

Kira mentally pushed again at Lara but nothing

happened. After the last psychic push the bitch had erected a shield around herself. Now Kira's only option really was to get the hell off the deck and make a run for it.

The next ball of energy Lara threw, Kira mentally pushed it to a nearby wooden table. On impact the table burst into flames, distracting Lara for a split second. Kira ran, her feet pounding against the wood and off the deck where she practically dove into the nearby tree line.

Lucas! Where the hell are you? I'm on the run from her and headed in a south, southwesterly direction from the back of the cabin. She frantically tried to touch Lucas' mind with all they power she had.

I'm almost there, baby. Just a few miles away. There's an unmarked densely covered path that will lead you straight toward the river. Follow it. We'll meet you there. Hurry.

Unbelievably, having him in her head soothed and centered her. Her focus seemed sharper and her body surged with power as she ran as hard as she could, her feet pounding the ground as fast as her heart raced.

Kira. Stay safe, baby. I can't lose you.

She ran, enjoying the flow of power through her when suddenly she was jerked from the path. Someone had grabbed her arm and yanked her down as she passed. Stubby fingers dug into the flesh of her arm, pushing her into the grass face first.

The sheer force of being grabbed from a dead run and then flung to the ground caused a sharp wave of nausea to rise in her throat. Gasping for breath, she took in deep gulps of air in the hopes of finding her equilibrium fast. She yanked her arm free, swiveling quickly onto her back to get a good look at who had grabbed her.

Realization dawned as the true betrayal in this scenario began to sink in. "Lawrence, what the fuck are *you* doing here?"

Hell, was there any chance she was wrong about him and he'd just tried to save her? She rubbed her arms furiously, trying to ease the ache from his surprisingly strong grip. "You could have hurt me." Despite the nausea threatening to take her down again, she sprang up ready to run. "We've got to get out of here now. There's a crazy assed black witch trying to kill me. We have got to hide from—" the words froze in her throat as she spotted his weapon.

"You're not going anywhere." He leveled a gun at her chest to make his point abundantly clear. "I've had enough of this bullshit. I should have known that if you want something done right, you have to do it yourself."

Something clicked in Kira's mind. Her stepfather stood before her holding a gun on her, not the least bit surprised to hear about Lara pursuing her. For years he'd made her skin crawl and now she truly knew why.

Pure evil could only hide so long before revealing itself. All along he had wanted her out of the way one way or another. He'd pushed for the council to end her 'suffering', then she'd gotten mated and stopped her decline. Apparently, the cold and loveless way he had treated her mother all these years wasn't enough. He had finally come for her too.

"Why are you doing this? What do you want from me?" She took a step back trying to put a little distance between herself and Lawrence's gun.

"Don't be a stupid little bitch. You know exactly what

this is about." He raised the gun a little higher. "Power. You have more than you deserve and I want it."

"What the hell are you talking about? How can you take my powers from me? I'm mated now. Killing me only takes them away from me."

"Come on, girlie, I thought you were brighter than that. Don't be so narrow minded." When Kira failed to respond he continued. "The black witch you already mentioned. She's my ace in the hole. Why else would I need someone else to help get rid of you?" he replied.

At the mention of her, Lara burst through the trees, stopping just shy of plowing over Lawrence. With her eyes blazing red and hair standing on end, she looked more like a woman gone way over the edge than a criminal partner.

"'Bout time you showed up. I guess you still can't even handle one little girl," he sneered at Lara.

He might be using Lara to take care of his dirty work, but he clearly thought her less than dirt.

"Can you put a spell on her to prevent her from using her psi powers? I can feel her connection with that cat and if we don't break that fast we're going to have a nasty little party here before we're ready."

Lara's expression was thunderous towards Lawrence and Kira held her breath, waiting to see what she would do. She prayed for a break.

To her surprise, Lara didn't move like she'd hoped. Instead, she did a quick chant and with a simply wave of her hand Lucas disappeared. Blocked from Kira's mind. She was on her own.

Panic like she'd never known welled up in her throat,

threatening to choke her. *Remember your training. Remember your training. Stay calm.*

"It's done. I've temporarily bound her powers. It's now or never because that spell won't hold her long. You do know what will happen when you kill her, right? With their powers now bound together, if one dies they both die. It's what will make them so powerful together. And I can't guarantee I can harvest any of it."

Kira gasped. That couldn't be right. She refused to believe such nonsense. Probably just the ramblings of a crazed witch hell bent on killing her.

"I could care less about her shifter. If he had followed the rules set up by the councils ages ago, he wouldn't be in this mess. As for my pain in the ass stepdaughter, for you sake you better hope you can get what I need. I saved your life, now I want my payment."

Lara said nothing, but Kira got the impression that this partnership stood on shaky ground, possibly giving her something she could work with.

Lawrence turned his gaze solely to Kira and he tightened the grip on his gun. "You're coming with us right now. I need to take care of this without any more interruptions."

Kira thought desperately for another solution. If they got her away from here, it would be all over for her.

"This isn't going to work," she said, hoping against hope to buy herself some time.

Where the hell was Lucas?

"Why wouldn't it? It's not the first time I've done it."

Kira gasped at the darkness those words implied. She'd

always known that somehow some way he'd changed her mother, but she had no idea it went this deep.

"You did this to my mother? But she's so strong."

He grinned. "That's what everyone was supposed to think. Mind control is a tricky thing wouldn't you say?" He shrugged. "At least I left her alive. You, I'm afraid, will not be so lucky."

Jesus. His insanity went beyond evil and straight into crazy. Panic threatened to choke Kira as she reached frantically for her mate all while trying to find an alternate solution to this mess.

Well, if she couldn't reach him mentally why not take the good old-fashioned way? Kira opened her mouth and released a bloodcurdling scream.

By the look on Lawrence's face, she half expected him to shoot her in the face just to shut her up. Instead he raised his arm and cold cocked her with the butt of the gun. As she crumpled to the ground in agony, everything around her faded away in slow motion.

She'd failed.

CHAPTER
THIRTY-SEVEN

Kira's screams reverberated through Lucas' head. He heard them mentally as well as physically. The pain of her fear ripped through his body as skin gave way to fur. His shift was instantaneous as well as uncontrolled.

He and Malcolm had been searching the area near the river for her when she screamed. With barely a glance to Malcolm, he sprinted after her. Blood thundered through his body as he raced to find her in time.

If even a hair on her head was hurt someone would die, slow and painful.

Lucas burst through the trees to find Lawrence dragging his unconscious mate by the hair. With nothing but blind fury in his mind, he leapt across the clearing to get to her before her stepfather had a chance to react. In one vicious move, Lucas sank his razor sharp teeth into Lawrence's arm and, with the sickening sounds of bones and cartilage popping, he crushed the man's arm, leaving it useless and unable to maintain a hold on Kira.

His bloodlust far from sated, he turned his attentions to the witch. She lifted her chin, meeting his angry gaze straight on as he stalked towards her. Electricity sparked from her fingertips as she prepared to strike at him.

She chuckled. "Fine by me you sick son of a bitch. You can be the first to pay. You Guardians judge innocents without a care to the consequences. Without a shred of proof. Now the not so innocent judges you." Her eyes glowed red as she prepared for battle. "Today is the day you die for your crimes as a Guardian."

Flinging her right arm at him, an energy ball came straight at his head. But he had the reflexes of the cat and easily avoided it by jumping out of its path. Too late, he realized his move left Kira exposed. Lara threw another ball at Kira, aiming for her heart. Lucas lunged across Kira to protect her just as the damaging energy hit his hind leg. He crumpled to the ground in front of Kira's body, still trying to cover her.

He wasn't dead but the damage was done. He couldn't move. His flesh and fur burned in white hot agony as his body shifted back to human form. A raw and primitive grief for Kira consumed him as he watched helplessly as Lara prepared her final blow.

Wake up, Kira! You've got to move.

Lara rubbed her hands together, creating a blast the size of a bowling ball. This one was strong enough to go through both of them at the same time if he wasn't mistaken.

When her arm cocked to deliver the final blow, she crumpled to the ground. Malcolm was left standing behind her holding a large tree branch he'd used to strike her down.

"About damn time you showed up." Lucas' tongue was heavy with sarcasm he didn't really feel. In reality he was grateful to once again have his brother's help.

Malcolm strode over to Lucas and surveyed the damage. After a few painful pokes and prods that must have satisfied him, he turned back to check on the others.

"What the hell? Where did she go?" Malcolm snarled.

They both searched the area. "She's worse than a cat with nine lives. Looks like she's disappeared on us again. Again." Lucas groaned. He hated loose ends.

"She'll be back. It sounds like she has a plan for us. Whatever the hell she thinks we've done, she's pissed."

"You're right about that, but she's not the only one." They jerked at the sound of Lawrence's voice and when Lucas turned he found the idiot had recovered the gun with his remaining good hand.

"You have got to be kidding." Lucas growled.

"Shut up or I'll put a bullet in each and every one of you." He turned and pointed the muzzle at Kira's head. "Starting with her."

That uncontrollable rage rushed through Lucas' veins once again. Bloodlust ate at his mind. Any threat to his mate had to be eliminated. His growls turned to fierce cries that echoed through the forest as he tried to crawl and cover his mate's still form.

"What the—" Lawrence took a few steps back looking frightened while still holding the gun on Kira. "Stop whatever you're doing or I'll kill her." His hand trembled and Lucas feared the gun would go off anyway.

Their screeching yowls continued. For he and his brother there was nothing left but animal instinct.

"God. Every disgusting rumor about you filthy creatures was true all along. I can't believe we have to share anything with—

Lawrence's tirade stopped when Malcolm pounced, gripping him with his claws and tossing him to the ground like a rag doll. No more words were uttered as his brother bit into the throat of the man who no longer deserved to breathe the air on this earth.

THIRTY-EIGHT

L ucas felt Kira watch him pace. The thought of nearly losing her in the woods while he was out goofing off still tormented him. His brothers had recently finished with their questioning in the council chambers and now they all waited to hear their fate. To say every minute was nerve-wracking was a massive understatement.

"Lucas, you're making me nervous." Her voice held a slight tremor when she spoke.

"I'm tired of waiting. It's taking them entirely too long to come to a decision. What more do they need? We answered every ridiculous question and then some. This is not a hard decision." He stared at the chamber door, willing someone to walk through it.

"You would never last five minutes in the military with your attitude." She laughed and the soft lilt of that sweet sound relaxed him a fraction. "Seriously, sometimes I think the entire military philosophy is built around *hurry up and wait*."

"That's not very logical."

"You have no idea." Again she spoke with a high voltage smile that lit up her face, transforming what could very well be a very bad day into a beautiful one. He was a damned lucky bastard to have her.

Desire arced between them as he stared down at her. They should be off alone somewhere doing what newly mated shifters do instead of wasting their time here on a group of grumpy old men steeped in traditions that no longer applied.

Their angry words and deep hatred still buzzed through his veins. Their fear of cross breeding remained intact as always and it seemed no exceptions would be made in his case. His status as Clan Guardian forced them to listen to what he said, but not all heard his words. Or cared.

Instead of thinking about the problem of their shrinking numbers and how to fix it, they were solely stuck in the past. Their system needed changes and it would either come from within or eventually the clans would fracture and a war would break out. Either way that wasn't happening today.

Which meant his priorities were changing as they stood here. No longer would Clan come first. His focus would be family and that would start with his beautiful mate. He didn't fully comprehend what the future looked like, but his instincts told him they'd be better off together.

He started toward her.

The door to the council chambers opened with a loud creak and Nick, Kane's childhood friend and Council mouthpiece, came sauntering out to them in the hall. "They will see you now."

Lucas looked down to his brothers, who both nodded at him. For the first time in a long time they would stand together despite some of the residual animosity between them. Facing Malcolm's role in the events that transpired would be difficult at best, but if they were all separated again now the rift would only grow, dividing them even further.

Malcolm and Kane filed into the room and Lucas turned to his mate. She looked at him with soft eyes filled with as much love as he felt. He had no choice but to tip his head down and press his lips gently to hers. A familiar spark fired as his tongue slid over her lips and her mouth opened on a small sigh. His senses filled with everything about her—her scent, her taste and her love. It was enough to bring a man to his knees.

"Come on, you two, you can get a room later," Nick interrupted.

Lucas reluctantly released Kira's mouth only to rest his forehead against hers.

"Whatever happens, we'll be okay," she reassured him despite the unease he sensed in her.

He nodded, grabbing her hand to follow Nick into the chamber. "We definitely will," he reassured her.

When he stepped inside, the whole room reeked with old world tradition. The walls were lined with tomes filled with centuries of Scottish history as well as their newer American history from the last century or so.

He'd never felt a draw to visit the homeland of his ancestry, but every time he'd entered this chamber in the past he'd experienced a surge of pride in all those pieces of history that had shaped them into what they were today.

Now he had doubt. Fate had delivered Kira as his mate and these nine men giving him cold, hard looks saw that as a bad thing. He would never agree with that. No one liked change no matter how it shaped history and he suspected this was only the beginning. There would be more change to come whether they liked it or not.

"We have come to a decision." Their leader delivered the simple statement in a cold, clipped tone. "In the case of Malcolm Gunn's role in recent events including the unauthorized death of Lawrence Reid: we find his actions in general revolting but his motivations somewhat understandable. We also took his ultimate involvement in the protection of our Guardian against Mr. Reid and others under advisement and have decided to wave the expected death sentence.

Relief swept through Lucas. Maybe there was hope.

"Instead he will continue his banishment as originally sentenced until this council decides otherwise."

Lucas started to protest. What the hell? Did they want a repeat of recent events? Kira squeezed his hand and a soft "don't" filtered through his mind. He didn't want to stand down, but he trusted his mate. He straightened his spine and resumed his blank and stoic appearance to the men in front of him.

"Secondly, in regards to the unfortunate and irrevocable mating between Lucas Gunn of Clan Gunn and Kira MacDonald of Clan MacDonald. We find you both have broken the covenant between clans and you both are ordered to banishment from the clan for a period of no less than one year. At which time the council will review the periodic medical tests you will be required to undergo to study the effects of combining your psychic powers. You will then reappear here for a secondary ruling at which time lifetime banning is still an option."

Lucas stood there stunned. One year and then another hearing? He had expected far worse, but still the immediate loss of guardianship stung.

"Furthermore, with the clan loss of its guardian, Kane Gunn will be appointed to take over the role from his brother."

The deafening silence in the room after the verdict made him twitchy, although he would never show it.

After a few more long tense minutes the leader stood. "Gentlemen, I suggest you all get your acts together and consider the clan repercussions of your actions from here on out. You won't like the outcome if we have to do this again."

One by one the Council filed out, leaving them to stand alone—but together.

AFTER THE COUNCIL MEETING, they'd gone in separate directions each needing time to deal with their fate. Lucas was grateful to be back home with Kira in the peace and quiet they needed as he struggled with his emotions.

Not only had mating caused their life forces to be linked, but their combined psychic powers were stronger than any documented. It was a little intimidating. He'd been further informed they would have to be extremely cautious until they learned how to develop and use their additional powers together. No wonder the Councils had always been so adamant about the races not mixing. These powers in the hands of a morally weak couple could wreak havoc on the clans as well as humans.

Under normal circumstances and with anyone else, their actions would have resulted in immediate and final banishment if not death by his hand. However, these weren't exactly normal times. He was still surprised the ruling elders would allow the two of them with their enhanced powers to leave. It downright baffled him.

Lucas stopped in his tracks at the far side of the cabin from Kira and turned back to face her.

God, he loved her. He needed to claim her. Again. Despite the fact they'd already been through the mating ritual, he still regretted it had been under duress. He wanted her to come willingly to him. His need built so strong until he thought his dick would rip through his jeans at any second. He throbbed with want to the point of pain. He needed her now.

So he stalked her. Slowly moving toward where she relaxed on his recliner. She looked so calm and serene while he was fighting to keep the animal on a leash. Except...

His nose caught the scent of his mate's heat. She was faking that calm exterior. He growled with pleasure, knowing he wasn't the only one who suffered. Without a word he scooped her up and carried her into the bedroom.

CHAPTER
THIRTY-NINE

L ucas wasted no time or words on getting them to the bed. He spread her legs as he came down on top of her, positioning for maximum pressure against her hard little clit.

"Lucas," she gasped. "We should talk. We have some serious logistics issues to figure out."

"No, baby. Right now I'm going to fuck you. You are mine and I am yours, but if I don't get inside you soon, I'm going to explode." With those words whispered in her ear, she writhed out of control trying to find some much needed friction between her legs. Her core clenched at the thought of him driving inside her, taking what he needed, when he needed it.

God, she loved him.

Leaving no more time for thought, he covered her lips with his and drove his tongue deep into her mouth to tangle with hers. He tasted of outdoors, musk and man. It drove her wild. She flexed her hips up, causing added pressure from his cock against her aching need.

"More. I want more," she begged. He grinned against her lips.

"I thought you wanted to talk."

"Shut up, Lucas."

"Then tell me, Kira. Tell me exactly what you want me to do to you and I'll do it." His tongue gently caressed and nibbled against her lips as he waited for her to tell him. The little nips shot sensations straight to her sensitive girl parts.

"I want you in my mouth so I can taste you again." Her hands roamed across his back and down to his muscled ass. Nails digging in, she encouraged him to rub harder. She so desperately wanted to be naked she was tempted to rip the clothes away from both their writhing bodies.

"I want you thrusting deep and hard inside me, filling me, taking me." She added, knowing he loved it when she talked dirty.

Winding her hands around the front of his lightly furred chest, she pushed him with all her strength, rolling him off of her and onto his back. Jumping off the bed, she frantically removed her shirt and pants, her taut nipples protruding through the thin lace of her bra, begging for freedom.

Lucas tossed his own clothes across the room as she stripped off the last scraps of lace. "Come on, baby. Get back on this bed so I can taste those gorgeous nipples."

Her body shivered at his words. She had a thing for the dirty talk too. The more he talked about what he wanted to do to her, the more heat flowed from her sex.

Slowly, she crawled up his body, positioning herself between his legs. She brought her mouth within an inch of his thick, glorious rod, but instead of taking him into her mouth, she gently blew on him. He bounced against her lips in reaction.

"No teasing today," he said, growling. "Suck it." His voice was hoarse with need and she responded by flicking out her tongue and licking him from root to tip against the bulging vein and swirling around the deep, now plum colored head.

She was rewarded with a small bead of cum she greedily lapped at. The salty taste of his essence sparked an intense, driving need in her as she swallowed his length as far as she could. With his strangled moan, she got a strong mental push from him, lighting a fire inside her. Her nipples tingled from the onslaught. Hell, her whole body tingled. As she eased her mouth back, his hips bucked, trying to keep him in deep. She moaned around him.

"Suck it. Kira. Suck it harder."

With her methodic rhythm, his cock swelled and his blood raced through his veins underneath her tongue. Kira knew if she kept this up much longer he would come soon. As much as she loved it when he came in her mouth, she wanted to feel him inside her, stretching her to the limits of pleasurable pain.

It didn't surprise her when he read her thoughts, pulled her off him and lifted her up into his lap. The broad head of his erection rubbed her wet folds, spreading her moisture, from top to bottom, further preparing her for the coming invasion.

She couldn't take it anymore. So much need formed a hazy cloud of lust around them. She trembled. She'd go crazy if he kept this up.

"What happened to no teasing?" she asked, gasping for breath.

His only response was to position against her entrance, giving her the chance to push down and draw him into her on one hard thrust.

Her vision wavered as him stretching and filling her momentarily robbed her of air. *Yes, that was it.*

The intensity of the pleasure mixed with the slight pain of her body trying to accommodate his width blew her mind. His moans mingled with hers as they both fought to hold onto a thread of control.

"God, Kira. You're so fucking tight and hot around my dick," he panted.

Again his words stoked the flames within her. She bucked against him, trying to force him deeper still. The pleasure in her womb was building to an impossible level and she was close to her own release.

Without warning, Lucas grasped her around the waist and lifted her off of him. Twisting to the side. he her down on her hands and knees, before quickly moving behind her. There, he pulled her ass tight against his hips, and began the torturously slow but pleasure filled first slide inside her. By the time he was fully seated he'd already ignited an explosive orgasm.

As she convulsed around him, he drove in and out of her hard, slamming deeper each time. His magical touch extended her orgasm out beyond anything she'd ever experienced before.

His fingers stroked the back of her neck where he'd marked her, forcing a moan to slip past her lips. Her skin was on fire.

Leaning over her back, he whispered in her ear. "This time it's for real. Nature may have pushed us together, but today I freely give you my heart, Kira MacDonald." With those words racing through her mind, and her muscles milking him for all he had, he sank his canines into the sacred spot on her shoulder.

The quick surge of white-hot pain from his bite quickly subsided to pleasure as heat from her mate filled her.

Mindless to the pleasure now, she barely noticed him release her shoulder as he continued to thrust through his own orgasm. All of which pushed her into another earth shattering explosion.

His rumble of pleasure turned into a full-blown roar as he claimed her as his woman. Forever.

Hours later, she lazily watched Lucas prepare them dinner. She admired the aura of the handsome man who now belonged to her. He had put on a pair of jeans to come to the kitchen but had left his chest and feet bare. She gazed at his skin that had been bronzed by the sun, her fingers itching to caress his back as he'd done hers.

The depth of emotion that had poured from him and into her when he had mated with her again shook her. She had known that he cared for her, and God knew they both lusted after each other constantly, but when he bit her mark again, everything he felt had flowed into her in that white hot flash.

He had opened his soul to her and shared his inner-most thoughts with her. Memories of him and his brothers through the years, including the anguish he had suffered when he had been forced to banish his own brother. The loneliness he often felt as an isolated Guardian. Even the pain and fear he had experienced from all of her recent actions.

All of his actions thus far had proven him the man she could trust with her heart. She wanted to give him everything and see what happened. She needed to take the risk. If he ever tried to manipulate her, well, she'd just find a way to kick his ass.

She scooted towards him all the while watching the muscles in his back and arms flex with his movements. Her mouth watered. She wanted to taste his flesh again. But first she had to tell him how she felt.

Sliding their omelets on plates, Lucas turned towards the table nearly stumbling into Kira.

"Damn, woman. How do you manage to sneak up on me? No one else can come within fifty feet of me without my knowing." She merely stared, tongue-tied. "Let's eat, I'm starving." Still she didn't move or speak instead she was frozen by unfounded fear.

Snap out of it, Kira.

Her heart was racing, her palms sweating. "Kira, what's wrong, baby?" He set the plates down and looked at her with clear concern shining from his eyes. His genuine concern filled her with warmth, which she used to calm her racing heart. Once again his presence centered her.

"Lucas, I need to tell you something." She drew in a deep breath and forbade herself from trembling anymore. He looked at her patiently, waiting for her to say her peace.

"I love you," she whispered hastily.

He exhaled a long sigh of relief. "Is that all? Damn, you scared me to death there for a minute. By the look on your face I was expecting bad news." He gathered her in his arms pressing her cheek to his chest stroking her hair. "I love you, too." She gloried in the shared moment.

"I don't know how we are going to work through our problems with the Council or our unusual living situations, but I'm confident we can find some happy medium for everyone." She turned and pressed her lips to his nipple.

"We'll figure something out, darling. Now sit and eat before it gets cold." She eagerly bounced over to the table to check out his handiwork. "Since you keep making a habit of scaring the crap out me, I think it's high time I gave you a lesson in what to expect when you scare someone like me."

Part of her wanted to roll her eyes and mock his words. But there was something about the sexy drawl he used that had the implications of what he said making her grow hot. She'd probably let him do whatever he wanted as long as he kept looking at her like she was more important than his next breath.

That thought made her squirm. With as much innocence as she could muster, she turned back to him.

"Lesson? What kind of lesson?" she teased.

"Hurry up and eat and I'll show you." He sat across from her with a grin a mile wide. "I can't wait to get my hands on that fine ass again."

CHAPTER FORTY-ONE

T he next morning, Lucas stood on the deck with Kane, watching Malcolm approach the house, backpack slung over his shoulder.

"You leaving now?" He and Kane had been working their way to goodbye as Kira made last minute decisions on what to pack for California. With his banishment from the clan there was no reason for her not to return to her job in the Marines.

"The sooner the better, I think." Lucas regretted the separation between him and his brother, and didn't relish leaving Kane alone to protect the Dragon. It was a lot of pressure to put on all of them, let alone only one.

"I still can't believe the Council is forcing you and Kira to leave the Dragon. I'm getting tired of their ancient ways. It's past time for them to move into this century and face the fact we aren't out here alone anymore." Malcolm's voice held a note of resignation despite the heat in his tone.

Kane nodded his head. "This place has been the heart and soul for Lucas since he was a cub. We need him here."

"I'm not the only one." Lucas looked between both brothers then and the pain he felt was mirrored in their gazes as well. He couldn't lie and say all was forgiven between him and Malcolm, but their family ties ran too deep to ignore. He believed time would heal the wounds. Or at least that's what Kira kept trying to tell him.

"We'll be back. The Council promised to study all of the old mating laws over the next twelve months and then schedule an appeal for us at that time."

"I still say it's bullshit. Something has to be done." Kane's angry outburst troubled Lucas, but this time there wasn't a damn thing he could do to help. His brother would have to deal with the council on his own.

"It will all depend on how you focus your combined powers during that time. It's just a stupid test, which I have no doubt you will both pass."

"What about you, Mal, what will you do? The Council was really pissed about your part in this whole mess. You keep managing to find the worst kind of trouble. One of these days it's going to be your downfall."

"Damn it, Lucas, you know what I went through. I really thought I was dying. Being unable to shift caused unbearable physical pain. I lived with it for a very long time, but after a while it began to mess with my head."

"Well, now you have your abilities back and you can go back to your carefree lifestyle."

Malcolm visibly winced at Kane's obvious insult. "You're right, little brother, I only care about myself.

Always have and always will." Turning on his heel, he stalked back into the woods and out of their life once again.

Lucas looked over at Kane. "If it wasn't for him, Kira would be dead. No matter what he has done, I will never forget that."

Kane nodded. "I get that. But I still can't wrap my head around what he did and how he's suddenly better."

"I'm not so sure he is. Something happened out there that made him able to shift, but it wasn't the same. *He's* not the same. I think he's still hiding something."

"Would that surprise you? It wouldn't me." Kane dropped onto a bench and stared into the distance. "I wish I could leave, too. In fact I want nothing more than to hop on my Harley and ride out of the Dragon right along with you. It's what the council deserves."

"You can't." He grabbed his brother by the shoulder and squeezed. "Everyone is counting on you now." Lucas knew Kane's sense of right and wrong was so deeply ingrained they both knew he would stay and serve as the last Guardian of their family line. Push come to shove, he believed any of them would. Even Malcolm.

"Have you given any thought to the Council's warning?" he asked Kane. "The urgency in them expecting you to find a mate and start a family?"

Guardianship could only be passed on through family bloodlines and in order to do that, Kane would have to father a child soon.

"Yeah, right. First I need to get laid."

Lucas laughed out loud at the screwed up look of frustration on his brother's face. "Since when do you have problems in that department?"

He hesitated. "Boredom, I guess. Most of the damn she cats I've been fucking are hell bent on something serious and I don't have that kind of interest in any of them."

Not since she touched me. Her wild violet eyes searing straight to my soul.

Lucas' eyes widened at the sudden outburst from Kane in his head. "I heard that," he said, turning to Kane. You've met someone." It wasn't so much of a question as it was a statement. He could hear his brother arguing with himself, yearning to take the woman who occupied his thoughts.

"Get out of my head, asshole. You picking up that psychic shit from Kira is unnerving."

"Then tell me."

"I don't want to think about it. It's way wrong and I'll fight it to my last breath." Kane shook his head and looked away, but it was too late. Lucas had heard him think her name.

"Please tell me you aren't serious."

"Absofuckinglutely not! If I ever see her again, I'm planning to kill her for what she's done, not take her to bed. Let alone *mate* her."

A roar tore from Kane's throat, piercing the night as he shoved Lucas out of his head and walked into the woods on the same path Malcolm had taken.

Lucas didn't know what to think or do. It wasn't easy to see his brother in so much anguish. But that woman— No it had to be a mistake. She was definitely not the one.

Kane was the Guardian now. He had to hand out justice to all who earned it. But if he was already torn between duty and desire...

Goddess help them all if he runs across that woman again.

EPILOGUE

T*wo days later...*

LUCAS CLUTCHED Kira's fingers with one hand and the steering wheel of his rumbling muscle car with the other. It apparently didn't matter to him that a bright blue classic Charger might be a cop magnet like she'd suggested before they left the safety of the dragon. He'd insisted that a cross-country trek required an appropriate vehicle and her economical compact apparently wasn't it.

Watching him as she drove, she got it though. Lucas was hardly compact material. Quite the opposite actually. With well over two hundred pounds of muscle packed on his frame, her big man needed room to stretch. Him driving his car also gave her all the time to study him.

Since they'd met there had only been rare moments of quiet where she could simply observe or attempt a normal conversation with him. However, despite the whirlwind of time, or maybe because of it, she'd learned something more important.

How he reacted under pressure. Those reactions gave her more insight to the man than a thousand conversations ever could. He fought when he needed too, but he also took time to think before he reacted. She imagined years of meting out council justice had honed his responses to any number of high stress situations.

All of which might have left another man broken.

Now they were racing down the highway on their way to California, which might as well have been another world for their kind.

However, duty called and she still had another eighteen months on her current contract with the Marines. And since they'd been banished from both their clans, returning to base became imminent.

At least they had somewhere to go and somewhere to live--albeit far away from Lucas' home. A twinge of guilt had taken up residence in the back of her mind, nagging at her that his loss was all because of her.

"What is it?" he asked.

"What's what?"

"You've obviously got something on your mind, babe. You're frowning and that little wrinkle in your forehead is popping out. So go ahead and spit it out. What is it?"

She yanked down the passenger side visor and flipped open the mirror to examine her face. "I do not have wrinkles."

"You do when you scrunch up your face. That only happens when something is bothering you." He looked over at her and laughed. "Or when you frown at me apparently."

"It's not what you think. I'm not upset..." She let her words trail off because it wasn't easy to admit, even to the man she loved, that she felt responsible for his loss. The council decision could have been worse, but that fact gave her little comfort.

"Kira," he said, a clear tone of warning infused in his voice. "I thought we were past this."

She shrugged. Clearly he knew her mind as well as she did. "I can't help it. I want to shake it, I really do, but it's still there in the back of my stupid head. You didn't deserve this to happen to you."

"I don't deserve to wake up to the woman I love every single morning for the rest of my life?"

Her heart stuttered and her belly flipped on his words. It still surprised her how easily he came up with the right thing to say in every situation.

"Or maybe you think I don't deserve a beautiful, intelligent and sex starved woman in my bed."

That gave her a tingle. He always managed to do that too. "That's not what I meant." She hesitated. "And I'm not sex starved."

A low growl emanated through the cabin of the car and the vehicle began to slow until Lucas pulled to the side of the road and put the car in park. He swiveled toward her and had her grasped by the shoulders and pulled half way into his lap before she could gasp.

"Listen to me Kira and listen good this time," he said on a deeper growl. "I got exactly what I wanted. And there is absolutely no where else in the world I'd rather be than here with you right now in this car," he paused. "Except maybe in a bed so I could punctuate my words with my hand on your ass. But, we'll revisit that when we get to California."

She bit her bottom lip to keep from smiling. The man definitely had a thing for her backside and always wanting to swat it. "A little spanking therapy?" she asked, no longer able to hide her smile.

He growled again, knowing full well what that sound did to her. The tingling sensations increased until her toes began to curl from it. If she wasn't already trapped between his body and the hard steering wheel pressed into her hip, she'd be clamping her legs together to stem the effect of that growl.

"For you? Definitely, babe. You might as well add it as a regular thing to that little pocket calendar you like to write everything in."

"That's--"

"Don't even try it. You get off on it and we both know it."

She rolled her eyes. Even if it was a totally true state-ment that didn't mean she had to verbally agree.

Lucas kept going. "Our elders are assholes, but I'm okay with that. Do you know why? Because we're together. At the end of the day that's all that really matters. You and me, babe—together. That's all I need. Are you with me?"

She nodded her head. "Yeah." So much more than he knew. Fate had been a bitch to reckon with, but that didn't change how she felt.

"No more frowning?" he asked.

She shook her head. "Not about that."

It was his turn to frown. "What then? What else is happening in that busy brain of yours?"

"We're going to need a place to live. I can probably get us into some temporary quarters on base, but that won't last long. And we don't qualify for anything permanent. Our mating laws won't work with the humans."

"So we'll get a place nearby. I'd rather have something more private anyway. How close are you to the beach? I haven't seen one of those in a long time. And we'll need a little land too. The beastie doesn't play very nice if I don't take care of him too."

She compressed her lips into a thin line. This was getting more complicated by the second. "Well..."

"Spit it out."

She exhaled. "Beach front property in California is insanely expensive. And sadly, my military pay isn't going to cut it."

A clipped bark of laughter erupted from Lucas. "That's what you're worried about? Money?" He shook his head. "Babe."

Uncomfortable with the current subject, especially since her clan had cut her off financially, Kira tried to wiggle away from him. He simply gripped her tighter to keep her in place. "I know. It's a shitty way to bring it up. But I keep crunching numbers and it's going to be a stretch. Hell, a lot more than a stretch. It's going to be impossible."

"No. It's not. I've got this no problem." He brushed his thumb across her cheek. "I've got more than enough money for whatever we need. For all the council's stupid ideas and the ancient laws they want enforced, they pay really well. Over the years, I haven't needed all that much of what I've earned. So I saved it for a rainy day."

"It doesn't rain where we're going," she said, still absorbing the fact he was either loaded or had no clue what kind of money she was talking about.

He quirked his lips. "You know what I mean, Kira."

She ignored his warning. "Do you really know what kind of money I'm talking about?"

His hands released her arms and instead grabbed her face, pulling her even closer. Now face-to-face with him and his scent filling her head, some of her brain's concentration faltered. It was enough to send a tingle curling through her abdomen. Maybe he was right and she actually was sex starved.

He shook his head. "The more you talk, babe, the more spank debt you rack up. Keep this up and it's going to be a long drive for you this week with a sore ass."

A wicked sort of grin crossed his face that only made the tingling in her lower body worsen.

"Of course I know what kind of money it takes to live in California," he continued. "I may live in the woods, but I'm not some sort of heathen. I have satellite television *and* Internet. And I don't hide my money in my mattress either. I've been growing my financial portfolio for a long damn time. There's more than—"

"No!" she screeched, covering his mouth with her hand. "Don't say it. I don't want to know."

"Why the hell not?" he asked. "We're in this together now. Mates, remember? Besides, how else are you going to get it through that thick head of yours that you have nothing to worry about?"

"I don't know. Take your word for it? I just don't feel ready for that kind of information. My brain is already on overload."

He started laughing, a wonderful rich sound that always made her stomach flip when she heard it. "There's more then," he said, pressing a gentle kiss to her mouth before he nipped at her lower lip. "I've been doing something of my own."

"Can't it wait?"

He shook his head. "No, babe. It can't." This time he licked the seam of her lips and she opened to him as he took her deep with a kiss guaranteed to scramble her brains.

When they broke free, she struggled to catch her breath again.

He placed his forehead against hers and smiled. "We're going to get married too."

She blinked, certain she'd misunderstood. "What?"

"You said it yourself. You live in the human world where we can't exactly explain to people that we're mates. So we're going to get married. That will work for the military, yes? That's what they need."

"But—"

He placed his fingers on her lips. "Breathe, baby. Don't stress out. I've got your back. Humans use marriage to express their devotion and to make things legal in their world. I think it will be fun. Plus, we can use it as an excuse to go on a honeymoon somewhere warm and I can work on making you less sex starved."

She pushed at his chest and got exactly nowhere. They

were still both pinned between the steering wheel and the driver's seat.

"Oh my God! I. Am. Not. Sex. Starved. You have to quit saying that."

More laughter erupted from him and honestly, she caught it deep. Something she'd never truly believed in. Heat spread through her chest and despite his instance to the contrary, it had nothing to do with how badly she wanted him right now.

Okay, maybe a little.

But the truth of the matter was, she was literally going to marry the man of her dreams. People wrote fiction about that kind of thing and it had happened to her in real life.

"You're doing it again," he pinched her arm and pulled her instantly back to the present.

"I can't help it. My mother spent her whole life believing in this kind of thing and all along I thought she was crazy for it. It made her vulnerable and easy prey to people like Lawrence who only wanted to use her for her power."

Lucas' fingers flexed on her shoulder as he leaned forward and pressed a soft kiss to her lips. "And you were scared I'd be like him?"

For a moment her stomach dropped and a wave of regret washed over her. "Not now I'm not. But in case you haven't noticed, I'm a little thick headed when it comes to this kind of thing. I needed time even though I didn't have it."

"A little?" he asked a new smile creeping across his face. "Baby, if you were anymore stubborn—"

"Maybe you should shut up and kiss me before you

finish that sentence," she warned. "You know, quit while you're ahead."

Fortunately for them both, Lucas must have agreed, because he tipped his head and pulled her forward with the grip he had on the back of her neck until their lips crashed together.

She had dreamed of a man she thought needed rescuing, when it turned out they both did. Fate may have brought them together, but it was the man who made her feel everything again.

And if she had learned nothing else, she knew this feeling was something worth fighting the whole world for.

Three months later...

Lucas stood in the doorway to a back deck that overlooked the ocean, watching his wife soaking up the late afternoon sun.

Wife.

He mulled over the word he still wasn't used to. He really did prefer the word mate. But for both their sakes he'd focus on the human version of what she was to him.

Since neither of them were familiar enough with the traditional wedding protocols humans preferred, they'd opted to take the quick and easy route with an early morning trip to the local courthouse.

Funny thing, what had started out as a technicality had taken a deeper route as they pledged their commitment in front of witnesses. By the time they got to the ring exchange, he had to wipe the tears of joy from his beautiful mate's cheeks.

She was twisting at the gold band on her finger again. Sometimes she did that when she was nervous and others just because.

He'd been smart to suggest they get married. Not only so they'd fit into her current world better, but also because it had somehow cemented something else for her. The mating connection he felt with her had only grown stronger with each passing day since then as did their psychic power.

Even now he could listen in to her thoughts if he chose to. He didn't. Because he didn't need to. Her body betrayed her instead.

Like him, she ran hot almost all of the time. In fact, the cool ocean air was a blessing at times like these. He wanted her all of the time. He loved to tease her about being insatiable, when in reality she had nothing on him. Even now, after already having had her twice this morning he needed her again.

"Are you going to stand there all day watching me or are you going to join me?"

He smiled. Her senses were growing sharper. In fact, he'd started journaling the changes that occurred between them. The effect of their psychic bond as well as their mating bond.

"I'm not allowed to simply enjoy the view sometimes?" he said, his voice rougher than he'd expected.

She turned and looked up at him as he rounded her chair. "Is it the view that's got you broadcasting sexual suggestion in my brain? I mean the ocean is nice and all, but it's hardly a sexual turn on."

"Who said I was looking at the ocean?" He straddled her lounge chair and leaned down until his mouth hovered at the bare curve of her neck.

She laughed, a light melodic sound that went straight to his dick.

"Still think I'm the insatiable one?"

"Damn straight. I can't help it if my body responds every time you touch that ring and think about me. It's nature, baby. You're mine and I like that you know it."

She rolled her eyes. "Uh huh. That's you poking around in my brain, searching for my secrets. Don't think I don't know what you're doing."

"Maybe it's just the fact we live in paradise," he said, licking at her soft skin. "You have the taste of ocean on you and it's really good."

"You don't miss home?" she asked.

He lifted his head at the almost imperceptible tremor in her voice. Anyone else would not have noticed. He shook his head. "Not at the moment. Do you know how cold it is back there?"

She laughed, looking up at the warm sunshine. "I can imagine."

"Besides, Kane and Malcolm are a little busy right now. They don't need me underfoot. And as for the council—" He resumed licking her, making sure to brush against the swell of her breast peeking above the curve of her tank top. "Those bastards can kiss my ass. We'll go home when it's time to do something about them. Until then," he paused, lifting her shirt and exposing more of the lush body he loved. "I'm going to take care of my wife."

And he did. Because she loved being called his wife and he'd do anything for his mate.

He smiled. Even if it took the rest of their life together to satisfy her.

Thank you so much for reading!

You can experience more Southern Shifters and the revelation of Kane in MATE NIGHT, available now, and find out what happens when he catches the woman who's become his obsession.

Visit ElizaGayle.com for More Information

About Mate Night

Enemies become lovers, tempting fate, testing trust, and satisfying an undeniable need.

Keep turning the page for the first chapter of *Mate Night*, the next book in the Southern Shifter series!

If you want the complete information on all of the books in my Southern Shifters series, you can find the full reading order and links at ElizaGayle.com

BONUS CHAPTER

MATE NIGHT
(Book 2 in the Southern Shifter Series)
By Eliza Gayle
Copyright 2011

Kane opened the door to a wave of thick white smoke, stale grease, and Ted Nugent warbling from an ancient jukebox in the corner. He stood just inside the door and let his eyes adjust to the atmosphere. Even with his enhanced vision it still took a second to get used to the haze and dim interior of the bar. Although he used the term *bar* loosely.

It technically qualified because of the long serving bar along the back wall, with the various tequilas, vodkas and Scotches filling the shelves behind it. But the layer of grime and stench in this place would only draw drunks and skanks of which were plentiful in this town, from what he'd seen so far. He crossed the room and took the only available stool at the bar. He lifted his hand to the bartender who eventually ambled over.

"What can I get ya?"

"Scotch neat." He figured it would be the safest thing to order in a place like this.

Hell, when did I become such a snob?

While he waited for his drink he looked into the mirror on the wall behind the liquor to observe the men who were lined up at the bar on either side of him. Men of various ages in different degrees of grubby wear, but no one who really stood out. He tried to catch the gaze of each and every one of them, looking for one who might be willing to talk to him.

The bartender returned and slid a drink in front of him. "Anything else I can get ya? You want a menu?"

"No thanks, I'm just here waiting on someone." That nugget of information seemed to perk up the man's attention. His eyes glinted in the dim light and his head tilted toward Kane in apparent curiosity.

"Who you waitin' for? I know just 'bout everyone who comes in here."

"I'm waiting for a woman."

The bartender snorted before his face split into a big grin, revealing broken and yellowed teeth. He imagined the fights that broke out in this kind of place would eventually lead to a man's teeth being damaged and more.

"Not a lot of women come in here."

"Oh yeah, why's that?" The guy's smirk aggravated him. Either that or this hunt was beginning to wear thin.

"Not a lot of women come in here on a count of Twin Peaks next door. They either go over there to pick up the men getting horny watching the girls dance or they don't come within five miles of the place because they don't want to be caught dead near a titty bar."

Kane laughed at the statement he understood all too well. He'd spent his fair share of time in those bars and more. He'd even let his brother Malcolm drag him to a few fetish clubs when they were younger. But some of those clubs would be considered high class compared to this one; so yes, he could well imagine not a lot of women wanting to come near the place.

"I get your point." He took a swallow of his drink and allowed the slow burn in his throat and belly to comfort him. The liquor wasn't quite as smooth as he liked it but he couldn't complain, it would get the job done.

"So this girl of yours, she got a name?"

"Yeah, she does. It's Lara. I haven't seen her in a few weeks, and I'm looking forward to catching up."

The bartender winked knowingly at him. He had no idea. Kane wanted to find her so he could kill her and go back home, maybe then he could get her out of his head. Plus it was never good for a guardian to stay gone so long. If word got out the clan wasn't as protected, it could leave them open to attack or at the very least harassment from neighboring clans.

Before he could continue his conversation with the idiot behind the bar a man stumbled through the door, yanking Kane's attention in that direction. He was obviously drunk off his ass, but it wasn't his state of inebriation that had Kane on edge, it was his scent. The man reeked all the way across the room and the smell had Kane seeing red as he gripped the wooden edge of the bar to keep himself from ripping out the stranger's throat.

He was covered in the woman's scent. *Lara*. A low growl rumbled in his throat and the bartender shot him a questioning glance. Kane turned away from the door and ground his teeth to hold in the anger. Fur rippled along his skin and his fingers underneath the lip of the bar edge partially shifted to paws and claws as he scraped into the wood.

Kane caught a glimpse of himself in the mirror and willed his body to calm. Shifting out in the open was strictly forbidden and could heap a helluva lot of trouble on him and his kind that they couldn't afford to deal with right now. Not with both of the other guardians shunned from the clan. He sighed. He missed his brothers and it frustrated the fuck out of him that they were both gone. Especially Lucas. Being shunned for mating with a non-shifter just didn't seem right. She carried his mark, for Christ's sake. Sometimes who you end up with can't always be controlled. *Yeah, keep telling yourself that.*

Another glance in the mirror showed a man not as close to the edge as a few minutes ago. He breathed in deep, letting his lungs fill before slowly releasing the air. He no longer scratched at the bar with claws and he raised his hand to wipe the sweat that had broken out on his forehead.

He should be happy someone in the bar carried her scent, it meant he was getting closer. About fucking time. But the rage, where the hell was that coming from?

The man seated next to him threw some bills on the bar and walked out, leaving an open stool the new drunk guy immediately opted to occupy. Kane's groin tightened with the onslaught of Lara's scent and for once he wished he didn't have heightened senses. His body ached and thoughts of her were even more vivid than they had been in his dreams over the past nights. He had come to dread the time he had to sleep because he always dreamt of her.

Not as the vicious bitch he knew her to be. Oh, no. In his dreams Lara was a lush, naked temptress that he ached to get his hands on. He thought about licking each and every sweet inch of her night after night.

"Bartender, bring me a drink. Something strrrrong." The man slurred his words as he ordered but it brought him back to the present. It was the man sitting next to him, a stranger, not the woman.

He had a job to do and it appeared his luck had finally turned. He had a lead on finding her in the form of a young and stupid drunk.

Kane took another swallow of his drink and grimaced this time over the burn. He would sit here and finish his shitty Scotch and wait. Either this man would start talking or Kane would make him talk when he left the building. He struggled not to groan when some Credence Clearwater poured from the dusty old Juke in the corner.

Could this place be more stereotypical if it tried? He didn't think so.

When the bartender laid down a shot of tequila in front of the man, he picked it up and turned to Kane. "Here's to good alcohol and hot women."

At the man's words, Kane felt an honest to God tick in his eye and an overwhelming urge to smash his glass into the man's face and wrestle him down to the ground. Somehow he resisted.

"Here, here." He raised his glass in a mock toast. After they had both taken several more drinks he opted to move in. "Have a good night with a good woman then?"

"Hell yeah, I did. Fine piece of ass if I do say so myself." Kane had to bite his tongue as hatred for this man burned through his veins. He had asked for it so the least he could do is play along.

"Lucky man. I'm waiting on my girl now. Your girl got a name?"

The man hesitated with the rim of the glass perched on his bottom lip. His eyes were bloodshot as hell and glazed over to the point he wondered how the man could see in front of his face.

"Yeah—uhm—" He hesitated after every word. "She does or she doesn't?" "Well, I'm sure she does, but for the life of me I can't remember what it was." He snorted as he pelted down the last of his tequila. His face screwed up at the taste and Kane wondered for a moment if he was going to throw up. Either way he was prepared to move fast.

"Well, bud, I'm not sure whether that's good or bad. Guess it depends on if you want to see her again. A woman doesn't like a man who can't remember her name." Kane swallowed his own urge to vomit at this lowlife who sure as hell didn't deserve to even breathe the same air as Lara let alone fuck her.

Whoa, where the hell did that come from?

His words must have hit home as the man turned away from him and called after the bartender again. He even turned to his other side and struck up a conversation with the man sitting there. Damn it!

This wasn't going to work. He obviously couldn't play nice and the longer he sat there the stronger the urge became to kill him and put him out of everyone's misery.

Kane threw down some bills and headed to the parking lot. He could either wait outside and take care of things the old fashioned way or go next door and wait in the strip club. Either way he was out of there.

Kane paced along the tree line that surrounded most of the bar parking lot. Two hours had passed and the little shit had yet to come outside. He had leaned against the building wishing for a cigarette, sat in his Jeep listening to some rock music, and when he finally tired of doing nothing he hit the edge of the woods and shifted. The brush was dense and the parking lot not all that well lit, so it was easy for him to hide without losing sight of the entrance doors to both clubs.

More than once he'd considered the *other* club. He could slip in, find a nice girl to take him home, and maybe then he would finally stop having all those fucked up thoughts about a woman with a death wish. Strippers were usually a lot of fun, always willing to try new things. Not so uptight like most of the feline bitches in his clan.

A couple of times the door of the club had opened and he'd gotten a glimpse of naked flesh wrapped around a silver pole, long dark hair that brushed the ground with every dip, and long long legs that seemed to go on and on. He shook his muzzle. Yeah, he needed an outlet real bad.

A run would help. It wasn't as if this idiot would be

hard to track later. But he wanted to talk to him now, while her scent was fresh. Kane would give him another ten minutes and then he was going in. He took a few more minutes to enjoy the cool grass underneath his paws, he even scratched at the tree, stretching his legs and sharpening his already lethally sharp claws.

He envisioned being back in human form and he thought of Lara. His body shifted from cougar to human and he looked at himself. It irked him to see his arousal jutting out from his hips. He couldn't understand how thoughts of the woman he'd been sent to kill could make him harder than he'd ever experienced in his life. It wasn't right to want to fuck the woman who'd been trying to kill his brother for weeks. The day Lucas had left the clan he'd received orders to hunt her down and eliminate her. The council didn't like the idea of a witch on the loose who was not only willing and able to use black magic, but had made several attempts on the Guardians. An offense punishable by death.

Yet every time he closed his eyes he saw images of her. He couldn't deny she was a beautiful woman, even with the constant scowl she had on her face when looking at him or his brothers. But the eyes, well, they haunted him day and night. She may have been a tough bitch, but if the eyes are supposed to be the windows to the soul, then she hid far more about her than what she allowed on the surface.

He'd seen flashes of anger, distrust and pain, but there had been even more if he wasn't mistaken, and his instincts usually weren't. She hated them and he wanted an answer to that. Hatred like he'd seen didn't come from nowhere. There was a lot more to her story and he planned to get to it sooner or later. Once he captured her, the council could afford to wait a few days for him to carry out her sentence. He would have his answers first.

He crossed over to the rock he'd stowed his clothes behind and donned his jeans, buttondown shirt, and shit kickers. His patience had run out and it was time to go inside and drag the little fucker outside. He stalked across the parking lot once again and the door popped open, and the man Kane had been waiting for stumbled out. If he'd thought the man was drunk a couple of hours ago he was positively loaded now. This wasn't going to be any fun. While he'd been spoiling for a fight, the stumbling, bleary-eyed man could barely walk let alone take him on. Still, when Lara's scent overpowered the reek of alcohol and sweat, rage bubbled in his blood. This man had done more than just touch her, and for that he should die. She was his.

Fuck! He couldn't keep having stray thoughts like that. It wasn't right. She was a dead woman.

But first...

He grabbed the man by the collar of his shirt and threw him back against the building like a rag doll. The sound of his body crashing might have been loud, but Kane heard nothing beyond the blood rushing in his head. He let out a cry before pouncing against the guy pinning him to the wall.

"What the—" The man's eyes widened to huge orbs in his face. Shock glared from his face.

"Tell me about her." "Her? Her who? What the hell?" Kane shoved his arm across the man's throat and applied hard pressure against his windpipe, cutting off his air supply. "Do not fuck with me. Not if you want to wake up tomorrow to your pitiful existence in this shit hole town."

Hands frantically clawed at his forearm as the man struggled for breath, but Kane couldn't be budged. It would be so easy, even in human form, to just kill him. Precious seconds ticked by and he removed his arm, the man falling unconscious to the ground at his feet.

He grabbed him by the scruff of his neck and dragged him to the woods. This conversation would be best had in private and he didn't want to have to take care of someone else who might exit the bar at a really bad time.

He didn't have to walk far before he found a small clearing that even had some light from the near full moon above. He shook the man awake and had to restrain himself from laughing out loud at the fear written all over his face. Served the bastard right.

He took a few steps away. "Don't even think about running. You could never move faster than me and you'll just piss me off even more."

"What do you want from me? I don't have any money." Kane released a sigh of frustration.

"Focus, you idiot. This is not me robbing you. The girl. I want to know everything about the girl."

"What girl?"

Kane crossed back to the man in one big stride and slammed his fist into his face. The man cried out and stumbled back a few feet. His hand cradled his face as drops of blood ran from his nose.

"The girl whose scent is all over you. What do you know about her?"

The man hesitated. He was probably afraid to say the wrong thing.

"You mean the hot chick I met at Junior's earlier this evening?"

Kane glared, waiting for the man to go on.

"Why didn't you just say so, dude? I'm more than happy to pass on her information. She was all over me earlier tonight." When Kane made a move again towards him he raised his hands in resistance. "Whoa, hold on. It was the dance floor. We just danced. She your old lady or something?"

"Or something."

"Well, you might want to have a chat with her, 'cause she was all over every man there. Flirting and rubbing up against them. Hard to resist such a fine, fine woman, you know?"

Kane wondered if this idiot had any brain cells at all. It should have been obvious to anyone by now that he was holding onto control by a thread, yet the asshole kept babbling on about Lara in a way that incited him.

"Where is she?"

"I don't know. Last time I saw her was over at Junior's before he kicked me out. Stupid bastard, I wasn't even doing anything."

"Yeah, I just bet you weren't. Did she say anything at all to you?

"Just that she wanted to fu—" The man's few smarts must have finally kicked in or maybe the warning snarl that had escaped Kane's mouth unbidden woke him up.

"What else?"

291

"That's it. Really she wanted me to meet her at the Happy Hills Motel for some uhm—further discussion."

"Yeah, I'll just bet she did."

Luckily Kane already knew where the motel was. It sat just a few miles outside the center of town secluded in the woods except for the blinking sign out on the roadside. *Perfect.*

"Leave." The man stood frozen to the spot looking confused. "Leave now or die here." Kane's words finally sank in when the man shuffled past him and headed for the parking lot. Kane waited until he heard a car screeching before he dug into his jeans and pulled out his keys.

He had a bitch to corral.

Read more at elizagayle.com

ALSO BY ELIZA GAYLE

FIERCE

FURY

Bound by Magick:

UNTAMED MAGICK

MAGICK IGNITED

FORCE OF MAGICK

MAGICK PROVOKED

Single titles:

VAMPIRE AWAKENING

WITCH AND WERE

Writing as E.M. Gayle
CONTEMPORARY ROMANCE

Mafia Mayhem Duet Series:

MERCILESS SINNER

SINNER TAKES ALL

WICKED BEAST

WILLING BEAUTY

BROKEN SAINT

FALLEN ANGEL

Outlaw Justice Series:

SAVAGE PROTECTOR

RECKLESS PAWN

RUTHLESS REDEMPTION

Sins of Wrath MC:

CRUEL SAVIOR

SCORCHED KING

VICIOUS DEFENDER

Purgatory Masters Series:

TUCKER'S FALL

LEVI'S ULTIMATUM

MASON'S RULE